WITH A SWIRL OF THE SCREW THE ARROW SHOT OUT OF
THE WAY, CARRYING THE AERONAUT WITH HER.

Page 187

Tom Swift and his Motor-Boat.

AND

-BOAT

OR

THE RIVALS OF LAKE CARLOPA

BY
VICTOR APPLETON

AUTHOR OF "TOM SWIFT AND HIS MOTOR-BOAT," "TOM SWIFT AND HIS AIR-
SHIP," "TOM SWIFT AND HIS SUBMARINE BOAT," ETC

This book is from the:

santa clara
county
library district

APPLEWOOD BOOKS

Tom Swift® is a registered trademark of Simon & Schuster Inc.

The Tom Swift® Adventure Stories were originally published by Grosset & Dunlap. Applewood Books acknowledges the kind permission of Pocket Books, a Division of Simon & Schuster Inc., to reprint these books.

For further information about these editions, please write: Applewood Books, P.O. Box 365, Bedford, MA 01730.

10 9 8 7 6 5 4

Library of Congress Cataloging-in-Publication Data
Appleton, Victor, II.
    Tom Swift and his motor-boat, or, The rivals of Lake Carlopa / by Victor Appleton. —Facsimile ed.
        p. cm.
    Summary: Tom begins a new adventure on the day he purchases a damaged motorboat at auction and is threatened by a bully.
    ISBN 1-55709-176-5
    [1. Boats and boating—Fiction. 2. Adventure and adventurers—Fiction.] I. Title. II. Title: Rivals of Lake Carlopa.
PZ7.A653Mo   1992
[Fic]—dc20   92-29497
                                                   CIP
                                                    AC

TOM SWIFT AND HIS MOTOR-BOAT

BY

VICTOR APPLETON

AUTHOR OF "TOM SWIFT AND HIS MOTOR-CYCLE," "TOM SWIFT AND HIS AIR SHIP," "TOM SWIFT AND HIS SUBMARINE BOAT," ETC.

ILLUSTRATED

NEW YORK

GROSSET & DUNLAP

PUBLISHERS

CONTENTS

iii

TOM SWIFT AND HIS MOTOR-BOAT

CHAPTER I

A MOTOR-BOAT AUCTION

"WHERE are you going, Tom?" asked **Mr.** Barton Swift of his son as the young **man was** slowly pushing his motor-cycle out of the **yard** toward the country road. "You look as though you had some object in view."

"So I have, dad. I'm going over to Lanton."

"To Lanton? What for?"

"I want to have a look at that motor-boat."

"Which boat is that, Tom? I don't recall **your** speaking about a boat over at Lanton. What **do** you want to look at it for?"

"It's the motor-boat those fellows had **who** tried to get away with your turbine model **inven-**tion, dad. The one they used at the old **General** Harkness mansion, in the woods near the lake, and the same boat that fellow used when he got **away** from me the day I was chasing him here."

"Oh, yes, I remember now. But what is the boat doing over at Lanton?"

"That's where it belongs. It's the property of Mr. Bently Hastings. The thieves stole it from him, and when they ran away from the old mansion, the time Mr. Damon and I raided the place, they left the boat on the lake. I turned it over to the county authorities, and they found out it belonged to Mr. Hastings. He has it back now, but I understand it's somewhat damaged, and he wants to get rid of it. He's going to sell it at auction to-day, and I thought I'd go over and take a look at it. You see——"

"Yes, I see, Tom," exclaimed Mr. Swift with a laugh. "I see what you're aiming at. You want a motor-boat, and you're going all around Robin Hood's barn to get at it."

"No, dad, I only——"

"Oh, I know you, Tom, my lad!" interrupted the inventor, shaking his finger at his son, who seemed somewhat confused. "You have a nice rowing skiff and a sailboat, yet you are hankering for a motor-boat. Come now, own up. Aren't you?"

"Well, dad, a motor-boat certainly would go fine on Lake Carlopa. There's plenty of room to speed her, and I wonder there aren't more of them. I was going to see what Mr. Hastings' boat would

sell for, but I didn't exactly think of buying it.
Still——"

"But you wouldn't buy a damaged boat, would
you?"

"It isn't much damaged," and in his eagerness
the young inventor (for Tom Swift had taken
out several patents) stood his motor-cycle up
against the fence and came closer to his father.
"It's only slightly damaged," he went on. "I can
easily fix it. I looked it all over before I gave it
in charge of the authorities, and it's certainly a
fine boat. It's worth nine hundred dollars—or it
was when it was new."

"That's a good deal of money for a boat," and
Mr. Swift looked serious, for though he was well
off, he was inclined to be conservative.

"Oh, I shouldn't think of paying that much.
In fact, dad, I really had no idea of bidding at
the auction. I only thought I'd go over and get
an idea of what the boat might sell for. Perhaps
some day——"

Tom paused. Since his father had begun to
question him some new plans had come into the
lad's head. He looked at his parent and saw a
smile beginning to work around the corners of
Mr. Swift's lips. There was also a humorous
look in the eyes of the older inventor. He under-

stood boys fairly well, even if he only had one, and he knew Tom perfectly.

"Would you really like to make a bid on that boat, Tom?" he asked.

"Would I, dad? Well——" The youth did not finish, but his father knew what he meant.

"I suppose a motor-boat would be a nice thing to have on Lake Carlopa," went on Mr. Swift musingly. "You and I could take frequent trips in it. It isn't like a motor-cycle, only useful for one. What do you suppose the boat will go for, Tom?"

"I hardly know. Not a high price, I believe, for motor-boats are so new on our lake that few persons will take a chance on them. But if Mr. Hastings is getting another, he will not be so particular about insisting on a high price for the old one. Then, too, the fact that it is damaged will help to keep the price down, though I know I can easily put it in good shape. I would like to make a bid, if you think it's all right."

"Well, I guess you may, Tom, if you really want it. You have money of your own and a motor-boat is not a bad investment. What do you think ought to be the limit?"

"Would you consider a hundred and fifty dollars too high?"

Mr. Swift looked at Tom critically. He was

plainly going over several matters in his mind, and not the least of them was the pluck his son had shown in getting back some valuable papers and a model from a gang of thieves. The lad certainly was entitled to some reward, and to allow him to get a boat might properly be part of it.

"I think you could safely go as high as two hundred dollars, Tom," said Mr. Swift at length. "That would be my limit on a damaged boat, for it might be better to pay a little more and get a new one. However, use your own judgment, but don't go over two hundred. So the thieves who made so much trouble for me stole that boat from Mr. Hastings, eh?"

"Yes, and they didn't take much care of it either. They damaged the engine, but the hull is in good shape. I'm ever so glad you'll let me bid on it. I'll start right off. The auction is at ten o'clock and I haven't more than time to get there."

"Now be careful how you bid. Don't raise your own figures, as I've sometimes seen women and men, too, do in their excitement. Somebody may go over your head, and if he does, let them. If you get the boat I'll be very glad on your account. But don't bring any of Anson Morse's gang back in it with you. I've seen enough of them."

"I'll not, dad!" cried Tom as he trundled his motor-cycle out of the gate and into the country road that led to the village of Shopton, where he lived, and to Lanton, where the auction was to be held. The young inventor had not gone far before he turned back, leaving his machine standing on the side path.

"What's the matter?" asked his father, who had started toward one of several machine shops on the premises—shops where Mr. Swift and his son did inventive work.

"Guess I'd better get a blank check and some money," replied Tom as he entered the house. "I'll need to pay a deposit if I secure the boat."

"That's so. Well, good luck," and with his mind busy on a plan for a new kind of storage battery, the inventor went on to his workroom. Tom got some cash and his check book from a small safe he owned and was soon speeding over the road to Lanton, his motor-cycle making quite a cloud of dust. While he is thus hurrying along to the auction I will tell you something about him.

Tom Swift, son of Barton Swift, lived with his father and a motherly housekeeper, Mrs. Baggert, in a large house on the outskirts of the town of Shopton, in New York State. Mr. Swift had acquired considerable wealth from his many inventions and patents, but he did not give up working out his ideas simply because he had plenty of money. Tom followed in the footsteps of his parent and had already taken out several patents.

Shortly before this story opens the youth had become possessed of a motor-cycle in a peculiar fashion. As told in the first volume of this series, entitled "Tom Swift and His Motor-Cycle," Tom was riding to the town of Mansburg on an errand for his father one day when he was nearly run down by a motor cyclist. A little later the same motor cyclist, who was a Mr. Wakefield Damon, of Waterfield, collided with a tree near Tom's home and was severely cut and bruised, the machine being broken. Tom and his father cared for the injured rider, and Mr. Damon, who was an eccentric individual, was so disheartened by his attempts to ride the motor-cycle that he sold it to Tom for fifty dollars, though it had cost much more.

About the same time that Tom bought the motor-cycle a firm of rascally lawyers, Smeak & Katch by name, had, in conjunction with several men, made an attempt to get control of an invention of a turbine motor perfected by Mr. Swift. The men, who were Ferguson Appleson, Anson Morse, Wilson Featherton, *alias* Simpson, and Jake Burke, *alias* Happy Harry, who sometimes disguised himself as a tramp, tried several times to steal the model.

Their anxiety to get it was due to the fact that they had invested a large sum in a turbine motor invented by another man, but their motor would not work and they sought to steal Mr. Swift's. Tom was sent to Albany on his motor-cycle to deliver the model and some valuable papers to Mr. Crawford, of the law firm of Reid & Crawford, of Washington, attorneys for Mr. Swift. Mr. Crawford had an errand in Albany and had agreed to meet Tom there with the model.

But, on the way, Tom was attacked by the gang of unscrupulous men and the model was stolen. He was assaulted and carried far away in an automobile. In an attempt to capture the gang in a deserted mansion, in the woods on the shore of Lake Carlopa, Tom was aided by Mr. Damon, of whom he had purchased the motor-cycle. The men escaped, however, and nothing could be done to punish them.

Tom was thinking of the exciting scenes he had passed through about a month previous as he spun along the road leading to Lanton.

"I hope I don't meet Happy Harry or any of his gang to-day," mused the lad as he turned on a little more power to enable his machine to mount a hill. "I don't believe they'll attend the auction, though. It would be too risky for them."

As Tom swung along at a rapid pace he heard,

behind him, the puffing of an automobile, with the muffler cut out. He turned and cast a hasty glance behind.

"I hope that ain't Andy Foger or any of his cronies," he said to himself. "He might try to run me down just for spite. He generally rushes along with the muffler open so as to attract attention and make folks think he has a racing car."

It was not Andy, however, as Tom saw a little later, as a man passed him in a big touring car. Andy Foger, as my readers will recollect, was a red-haired, squinty-eyed lad with plenty of money and not much else. He and his cronies, including Sam Snedecker, nearly ran Tom down one day, when the latter was on his bicycle, as told in the first volume of this series. Andy had been off on a tour with his chums during the time when Tom was having such strenuous adventures and had recently returned.

"If I can only get that boat," mused Tom as he swung back into the middle of the road after the auto had passed him, "I certainly will have lots of fun. I'll make a week's tour of Lake Carlopa and take dad and Ned Newton with me." Ned was Tom's most particular chum, but as young Newton was employed in the Shopton bank, the lad did not have much time for pleasure. Lake Carlopa was a large body of water, and it would take a moderately powered boat several days to make a complete circuit of the shore, so cut up into bays and inlets was it.

In about an hour Tom was at Lanton, and as he neared the home of Mr. Hastings, which was on the shore of the lake, he saw quite a throng going down toward the boathouse.

"There'll be some lively bidding," thought Tom as he got off his machine and pushed it ahead of him through the drive and down toward the river. "I hope they don't go above two hundred dollars, though."

"Get out the way there!" called a sudden voice, and looking back, Tom saw that an automobile had crept up silently behind him. In it were Andy Foger and Sam Snedecker. "Why don't you get out the way?" petulantly demanded the red-haired lad.

"Because I don't choose to," replied Tom calmly, knowing that Andy would never dare to speed up his machine on the slope leading down to the lake.

"Go ahead, bump him!" the young inventor heard Sam whisper.

"You'd better try it, if you want to get the best trouncing you ever had!" cried Tom hotly.

"Hu! I s'pose you think you're going to bid on the boat?" sneered Andy.

"Is there any law against it?" asked Tom.

"Hu! Well, you'll not get it. I'm going to take that boat," retorted the squint-eyed bully. "Dad gave me the money to get it."

"All right," answered Tom non-committally. "Go ahead. It's a free country."

He stood his motor-cycle up against a tree and went toward a group of persons who were surrounding the auctioneer. The time had arrived to start the sale. As Tom edged in closer he brushed against a man who looked at him sharply. The lad was just wondering if he had ever seen the individual before, as there seemed to be something strangely familiar about him, when the man turned quickly away, as if afraid of being recognized.

"That's odd," thought Tom, but he had no further time for speculation, as the auctioneer was mounting on a soap box and had begun to address the gathering.

CHAPTER II

"ATTENTION, people!" cried the auctioneer. "Give me your attention for a few minutes, and we will proceed with the business in hand. As you all know, I am about to dispose of a fine motor-boat, the property of Mr. Bently Hastings. The reason for disposing of it at auction is known to most of you, but for the benefit of those who do not, I will briefly state them. The boat was stolen by a gang of thieves and recovered recently through the efforts of a young man, Thomas Swift, son of Barton Swift, our fellow-townsman, of Shopton." At that moment the auctioneer, Jacob Wood, caught sight of Tom in the press, and, looking directly at the lad, continued:

"I understand that young Mr. Swift is here to-day, and I hope he intends to bid on this boat. If he does, the bidding will be lively, for Tom Swift is a lively young man. I wish I could say that some of the men who stole the boat were here to-day."

The auctioneer paused and there were some murmurs from those in the throng as to why such a wish should be uttered. Tom felt some one moving near him, and, looking around, he saw the same man with whom he had come in contact before. The person seemed desirous of getting out on the edge of the crowd, and Tom felt a return of his vague suspicions. He looked closely at the fellow, but could trace no resemblance to any of the men who had so daringly stolen his father's model.

"The reason I wish they were here to-day," went on Mr. Wood, "is that the men did some slight damage to the boat, and if they were here to-day we would make them pay for it. However, the damage is slight and can easily be repaired. I mention that as Mr. Hastings desired me to. Now we will proceed with the bidding, and I will say that an opportunity will first be given all to examine the boat. Perhaps Tom Swift will give us his opinion on the state it is in, as we know he is well qualified to talk about machinery."

All eyes were turned on Tom, for many knew him.

"Humph! I guess I know as much about boats and motors as he does," sneered Andy Foger. "He isn't the only one in this crowd! Why didn't the auctioneer ask me?"

"Keep quiet," begged Sam Snedecker. "People are laughing at you, Andy."

"I don't care if they are," muttered the sandy-haired youth. "Tom Swift needn't think he's everything."

"If you will come down to the dock," went on the auctioneer, "you can all see the boat, and I would be glad to have young Mr. Swift give us the benefit of his advice."

The throng trooped down to the lake, and, blushing somewhat, Tom told what was the matter with the motor and how it could be fixed. It was noticed that there was less enthusiasm over the matter than there had been, for certainly the engine, rusty and out of order as it was, did not present an attractive sight. Tom noted that the man who had acted so strangely did not come down to the dock.

"Guess he can't be much interested in the motor," decided Tom.

"Now then, if it's all the same to you folks, I'll proceed with the auction here," went on Mr. Wood. "You can all see the boat from here. It is, as you see, a regular family launch and will carry twelve persons comfortably. With a canopy fitted to it a person could cruise all about the lake and stay out over night, for you could sleep on the seat cushions. It is twenty-one feet in length and has a five-and-a-half-foot beam, the design being what is known as a compromise stern. The motor is a double-cylinder two-cycle one, of ten horse-power. It has a float-feed carburetor, mechanical oiler, and the ignition system is the jump-spark—the best for this style of motor. The boat will make ten miles an hour, with twelve in, and, of course, more than that with a lighter load. A good deal will depend on the way the motor is managed.

"Now, as you know, Mr. Hastings wishes to dispose of the boat partly because he does not wish to repair it and partly because he has a newer and larger one. The craft, which is named *Carlopa* by the way, cost originally nine hundred dollars. It could not be purchased new to-day, in many places, for a thousand. Now what am I offered in its present condition? Will any one make an offer? Will you give me five hundred dollars?"

The auctioneer paused and looked critically at the throng. Several persons smiled. Tom looked worried. He had no idea that the price would start so high.

"Well, perhaps that is a bit stiff," went on Mr. Wood. "Shall we say four hundred dollars? Come now, I'm sure it's worth four hundred. Who'll start it at four hundred?"

No one would, and the auctioneer descended to three hundred, then to two and finally, as if impatient, he called out:

"Well, will any one start at fifty dollars?"

Instantly there were several cries of "I will!"

"I thought you would," went on the auctioneer. "Now we will get down to work. I'm offered fifty dollars for this twenty-one foot, ten horse-power family launch. Will any one make it sixty?"

"Sixty!" called out Andy Foger in a shrill voice. Several turned to look at him.

"I didn't know he was going to bid," thought Tom. "He may go above me. He's got plenty of money, and, while I have too, I'm not going to pay too much for a damaged boat."

"Sixty I'm bid, sixty—sixty!" cried Mr. Wood in a sing-song tone, "who'll make it seventy?"

"Sixty-five!" spoke a quiet voice at Tom's elbow, and he turned to see the mysterious man who had joined the crowd at the edge of the lake.

"Sixty-five from the gentleman in the white straw hat!" called Mr. Wood with a smile at his wit, for there were many men wearing white straw hats, the day being a warm one in June.

"Here, who's bidding above me?" exclaimed Andy, as if it was against the law.

"I guess you'll find a number going ahead of

you, my young friend," remarked the auctioneer. "Will you have the goodness not to interrupt me, except when you want to bid?"

"Well, I offered sixty," said the squint-eyed bully, while his crony, Sam Snedecker, was vainly pulling at his sleeve.

"I know you did, and this gentleman went above you. If you want to bid more you can do so. I'm offered sixty-five, sixty-five I'm offered for this boat. Will any one make it seventy-five?"

Mr. Wood looked at Tom, and our hero, thinking it was time for him to make a bid, offered seventy.

"Seventy from Tom Swift!" cried the auctioneer. "There is a lad who knows a motor-boat from stem to stern, if those are the right words. I don't know much about boats except what I'm told, but Tom Swift does. Now, if he bids, you people ought to know that it's all right. I'm bid seventy—seventy I'm bid. Will any one make it eighty?"

"Eighty!" exclaimed Andy Foger after a whispered conference with Sam. "I know as much about boats as Tom Swift. I'll make it eighty."

"No side remarks. I'll do most of the talking. You just bid, young man," remarked Mr. Wood. "I have eighty bid for this boat—eighty dollars. Why, my friends, I can't understand this. I ought to have it up to three hundred dollars, at least. But I thank you all the same. We are coming on. I'm bid eighty——"

"Ninety!" exclaimed the quiet man at Tom's elbow. He was continually fingering his upper lip, as though he had a mustache there, but his face was clean-shaven. He looked around nervously as he spoke.

"Ninety!" called out the auctioneer.

"Ninety-five!" returned Tom. Andy Foger scowled at him, but the young inventor only smiled. It was evident that the bully did not relish being bid against. He and his crony whispered together again.

"One hundred!" called Andy, as if no one would dare go above that.

"I'm offered an even hundred," resumed Mr. Wood. "We are certainly coming on. A hundred I am bid, a hundred—a hundred—a hundred——"

"And five," said the strange man hastily, and he seemed to choke as he uttered the words.

"Oh, come now; we ought to have at least ten-dollar bids from now on," suggested Mr. Wood. "Won't you make it a hundred and ten?" The auctioneer looked directly at the man, who seemed to shrink back into the crowd. He shook his head.

cast a sort of despairing look at the boat and hurried away.

"That's queer," murmured Tom. "I guess that was his limit, yet if he wanted the boat badly that wasn't a high price."

"Who's going ahead of me?" demanded Andy in loud tones.

"Keep quiet!" urged Sam. "We may get it yet."

"Yes, don't make so many remarks," counseled the auctioneer. "I'm bid a hundred and five. Will any one make it a hundred and twenty-five?"

Tom wondered why the man had not remained to see if his bid was accepted, for no one raised it at once, but he hurried off and did not look back. Tom took a sudden resolve.

"A hundred and twenty-five!" he called out.

"That's what I like to hear," exclaimed Mr. Wood. "Now we are doing business. A hundred and twenty-five from Tom Swift. Will any one offer me fifty?"

Andy and Sam seemed to be having some dispute.

"Let's make him quit right now," suggested, Andy in a hoarse whisper.

"You can't," declared Sam.

"Yes, I can. I'll go up to my limit right now."

"And some one will go above you—maybe Tom will," was Sam's retort.

"I don't believe he can afford to," Andy came back with. "I'm going to call his bluffs. I believe he's only bidding to make others think he wants it. I don't believe he'll buy it."

Tom heard what was said, but did not reply. The auctioneer was calling monotonously: "I'm bid a hundred and twenty-five—twenty-five. Will any one make it fifty?"

"A hundred and fifty!" sang out Andy, and all eyes were directed toward him.

"Sixty!" said Tom quietly.

"Here, you——" began the red-haired lad. You——"

"That will do!" exclaimed the auctioneer sternly. "I am offered a hundred and sixty. Now who will give me an advance? I want to get the boat up to two hundred, and then the real bidding will begin."

Tom's heart sank. He hoped it would be some time before a two-hundred dollar offer would be heard. As for Andy Foger, he was almost speechless with rage. He shook off the restraining arm of Sam, and, worming his way to the front of the throng, exclaimed:

"I'll give a hundred and seventy-five dollars for that boat!"

"Good!" cried the auctioneer. "That's the way to talk. I'm offered a hundred and seventy-five."

"Eighty," said Tom quietly, though his heart was beating fast.

"Well, of all——" began Andy, but Sam Snedecker dragged him back.

"You haven't got any more money," said the bully's crony. "Better stop now."

"I will not! I'm going home for more," declared Andy. "I must have that boat."

"It will be sold when you get back," said Sam.

"Haven't you got any money you can lend me?" inquired the squint-eyed one, scowling in Tom's direction.

"No, not a bit. There, some one raised Tom's bid."

At that moment a man in the crowd offered a hundred and eighty-one dollars.

"Small amounts thankfully received," said Mr. Wood with a laugh. Then the bidding became lively, a number making one-dollar advances.

The price got up to one hundred and ninety-five dollars and there it hung for several minutes, despite the eloquence of Mr. Wood, who tried by all his persuasive powers to get a substantial advance. But every one seemed afraid to bid. As for the young inventor, he was in a quandary. He could only offer five dollars more, and, if he bid it in a lump, some one might go to two hundred and five, and he would not get the boat. He wished he had secured permission from his father to go higher, yet he knew that as a fair proposition two hundred dollars was about all the motor-boat in its present condition was worth, at least to him. Then he made a sudden resolve. He thought he might as well have the suspense over.

"Two hundred dollars!" he called boldly.

"I'm offered two hundred!" repeated Mr. Wood. "That is something like it. Now who will raise that?"

There was a moment of silence. Then the auctioneer swung into an enthusiastic description of the boat. He begged for an advance, but none was made, though Tom's heart seemed in his throat, so afraid was he that he would not get the *Carlopa.*

"Two hundred—two hundred!" droned on Mr. Wood. "I am offered two hundred. Will any of you go any higher?" He paused a moment, and Tom's heart beat harder than ever. "If not," resumed the speaker, "I will declare the bidding closed. Are you all done? Once—twice—three times. Two hundred dollars. Going—going—gone!" He clapped his hands. "The boat is sold to Thomas Swift for two hundred dollars. If he'll step up I'll take his money."

There was a laugh as Tom, blushingly, advanced. He passed Andy Foger, who had worked his way over near him.

"You got the boat," sneered the bully, "and I s'pose you think you got ahead of me."

"Keep quiet!" begged Sam.

"I won't!" exclaimed Andy. "He outbid me just out of spite, and I'll get even with him. You see if I don't!"

Tom looked Andy Foger straight in the eyes, but did not answer, and the red-haired youth turned aside, followed by his crony, and started toward his automobile.

"I congratulate you on your bargain," said Mr. Wood as Tom proceeded to make out a check. He gave little thought to the threat Andy Foger had made, but the time was coming when he was to remember it well.

CHAPTER III

"WELL, are you satisfied with your bargain, Tom?" asked Mr. Wood when the formalities about transferring the ownership of the motor-boat had been completed.

"Oh, yes, I calculated to pay just what I did."

"I'm glad you're satisfied, for Mr. Hastings told me to be sure the purchaser was satisfied. Here he comes now. I guess he wasn't at the auction."

An elderly gentleman was approaching Mr. Wood and Tom. Most of the throng was dispersing, but the young inventor noticed that Andy Foger and Sam Snedecker stood to one side, regarding him closely.

"So you got my boat," remarked the former owner of the craft. "I hope you will be able to fix it up."

"Oh, I think I shall," answered the new owner of the *Carlopa*. "If I can't, father will help me."

"Yes, you have an advantage there. Are you

24

going to keep the same name?" and Mr. Hastings seemed quite interested in what answer the lad would make.

"I think not," replied Tom. "It's a good name, but I want something that tells more what a fast boat it is, for I'm going to make some changes that will increase the speed."

"That's a good idea. Call it the *Swift.*"

"Folks would say I was stuck up if I did that," retorted the youth quickly. "I think I shall call it the *Arrow.* That's a good, short name, and——"

"It's certainly speedy," interrupted Mr. Hastings. "Well now, since you're not going to use the name *Carlopa,* would you mind if I took it for my new boat? I have a fancy for it."

"Not in the least," said Tom. "Don't you want the letters from each side of the bow to put on your new craft?"

"It's very kind of you to offer them, and, since you will have no need for them, I'll be glad to take them off."

"Come down to my boat," invited Tom, using the word "my" with a proper pride, "and I'll take off the brass letters. I have a screw driver in my motor-cycle tool bag."

As the former and present owners of the *Arrow* (which is the name by which I shall hereafter designate Tom's motor-boat) walked down toward the dock where it was moored the young inventor gave a startled cry.

"What's the matter?" asked Mr. Hastings.

"That man! See him at my motor-boat?" cried Tom. He pointed to the craft in the lake. A man was in the cockpit and seemed to be doing something to the forward bulkhead, which closed off the compartment holding the gasoline tank.

"Who is he?" asked Mr. Hastings, while Tom started on a run toward the boat.

"I don't know. Some man who bid on the boat at the auction, but who didn't go high enough," answered the lad. As he neared the craft the man sprang out, ran along the lake shore for a short distance and then disappeared amid the bushes which bordered the estate of Mr. Hastings. Tom hurriedly entered the *Arrow*.

"Did he do any damage?" asked Mr. Hastings.

"I guess he didn't have time," responded Tom. "But he was tampering with the lock on the door of the forward compartment. What's in there?"

"Nothing but the gasoline tank. I keep the bulkhead sliding door locked on general principles. I can't imagine what the fellow would want to open it for. There's nothing of value in there. Perhaps he isn't right in his head. Was he a tramp?"

"No, he was well dressed, but he seemed very nervous during the auction, as if he was disappointed not to have secured the boat. Yet what could he want in that compartment? Have you the key to the lock, Mr. Hastings?"

"Yes, it belongs to you now, Mr. Swift," and the former owner handed it to Tom, who quickly unlocked the compartment. He slid back the door and peered within, but all he saw was the big galvanized tank.

"Nothing in there he could want," commented the former owner of the craft.

"No," agreed Tom in a low voice. "I don't see what he wanted to open the door for." But the time was to come, and not far off, when Tom was to discover quite a mystery connected with the forward compartment of his boat, and the solution of it was fated to bring him into no little danger.

"It certainly is odd," went on Mr. Hastings when, after Tom had secured the screw driver from his motor-cycle tool bag, he aided the lad in removing the letters from the bow of the boat. "Are you sure you don't know the man?"

"No, I never saw him before. At first I thought his voice sounded like one of the members of the Happy Harry gang, but when I looked squarely at him I could not see a bit of resemblance. Besides, that gang would not venture again into this neighborhood."

"No, I imagine not. Perhaps he was only a curious, meddlesome person. I have frequently been bothered by such individuals. They want to see all the working parts of an automobile or motor-boat, and they don't care what damage they do by investigating."

Tom did not reply, but he was pretty certain that the man in question had more of an object than mere curiosity in tampering with the boat. However, he could discover no solution just then, and he proceeded with the work of taking off the letters.

"What are you going to do with your boat, now that you have it?" asked Mr. Hastings. "Can you run it down to your dock in the condition in which it is now?"

"No, I shall have to go back home, get some tools and fix up the motor. It will take half a day, at least. I will come back this afternoon and have the boat at my house by night. That is if I may leave it at your dock here."

"Certainly, as long as you like."

The young inventor had many things to think about as he rode toward home, and though he was somewhat puzzled over the actions of the stranger, he forgot about that in anticipating the pleasure he would have when the motor-boat was in running order.

"I'll take dad off on a cruise about the lake," he decided. "He needs a rest, for he's been working hard and worrying over the theft of the turbine motor model. I'll take Ned Newton for some rides, too, and he can bring his camera along and get a lot of pictures. Oh, I'll have some jolly sport this summer!"

Tom was riding swiftly along a quiet country road and was approaching a steep hill, which he could not see until he was close to it, owing to a sharp turn.

As he was about to swing around it and coast swiftly down the steep declivity he was startled by hearing a voice calling to him from the bushes at the side of the road.

"Hold on, dar! Hold on, Mistah Swift!" cried a colored man, suddenly popping into view. "Doan't go down dat hill."

"Why, it's Eradicate Sampson!" exclaimed Tom, quickly shutting off the power and applying the brakes. "What's the matter, Rad? Why shouldn't I go down that hill?"

"Beca'se, Mistah Swift, dere's a pow'ful monstrous tree trunk right across de road at a place whar yo' cain't see it till yo' gits right on top ob it. Ef yo' done hit dat ar tree on yo' lickity-split machine, yo' suah would land in kingdom come. Doan't go down dat hill!"

Tom leaped off his machine and approached the colored man. Eradicate Sampson did odd jobs in the neighborhood of Shopton, and more than once Tom had done him favors in repairing his lawn mower or his wood-sawing machine. In turn Eradicate had given Tom a valuable clew as to the hiding place of the model thieves.

"How'd the log get across the road, Rad?" asked Tom.

"I dunno, Mistah Swift. "I see it when I come along wid mah mule, Boomerang, an' I tried t' git it outer de way, but I couldn't. Den I left Boomerang an' mah wagon at de foot ob de hill an' I come up heah t' git a long pole t' pry de log outer de way. I didn't t'ink nobody would come along, 'case dis road ain't much trabeled."

"I took it for a short cut," said the lad. "Come on, let's take a look at the log."

Leaving his machine at the top of the slope, the young inventor accompanied the colored man down the hill. At the foot of it, well hidden from sight of any one who might come riding down, was a big log. It was all the way across the road.

"That never fell there," exclaimed Tom in some excitement. "That never rolled off a load of logs, even if there had been one along, which there wasn't. That log was put there!"

"Does yo' t'ink dat, Mistah Swift?" asked Eradicate, his eyes getting big.

"I certainly do, and, if you hadn't warned me, I might have been killed."

"Oh, I heard yo' lickity-split machine chug-chuggin' along when I were in de bushes, lookin' for a pryin' pole, an' I hurried out to warn yo'. I knowed I could leave Boomerang safe, 'case he's asleep."

"I'm glad you did warn me," went on the youth solemnly. Then, as he went closer to the log, he uttered an exclamation.

"That has been dragged here by an automobile!" he cried. "It's been done on purpose to injure some one. Come on, Rad, let's see if we can't find out who did it."

Something on the ground caught Tom's eye. He stooped and picked up a nickle-plated wrench.

"This may come in handy as evidence," he murmured.

CHAPTER IV

TOM AND ANDY CLASH

EVEN a casual observer could have told that an auto had had some part in dragging the log to the place where it blockaded the road. In the dust were many marks of the big rubber tires and even the imprint of a rope, which had been used to tow the tree trunk.

"What fo' yo' t'ink any one put dat log dere?" asked the colored man as he followed Tom. Boomerang, the mule, so called because Eradicate said you never could tell what he was going to do, opened his eyes lazily and closed them again.

"I don't know why, Rad, unless they wanted to wreck an automobile or a wagon. Maybe tramps did it for spite."

"Maybe some one done it to make yo' hab trouble, Mistah Swift."

"No, I hardly think so. I don't know of any one who would want to make trouble for me, and how would they know I was coming this way——"

Tom suddenly checked himself. The memory of the scene at the auction came back to him and he recalled what Andy Foger had said about "getting even."

"Which way did dat auto go?" resumed Eradicate.

"It came from down the road," answered Tom, not completing the sentence he had left unfinished. "They dragged the log up to the foot of the hill and left it. Then the auto went down this way."

It was comparatively easy, for a lad of such sharp observation as was Tom, to trace the movements of the vehicle.

"Den if it's down heah, maybe we cotch 'em," suggested the colored man.

The young inventor did not answer at once. He was hurrying along, his eyes on the tell-tale marks. He had proceeded some distance from the place where the log was when he uttered a cry. At the same moment he hurried from the road toward a thick clump of bushes that were in the ditch alongside of the highway. Reaching them, he parted the leaves and called:

"Here's the auto, Rad!"

The colored man ran up, his eyes wider open than ever. There, hidden amid the bushes, was a large touring car.

"Whose am dat?" asked Eradicate.

Tom did not answer. He penetrated the under-brush, noting where the broken branches had been bent upright after the forced entrance of the car, the better to hide it. The young inventor was seeking some clew to discover the owner of the machine. To this end he climbed up in the ton-neau and was looking about when some one burst in through the screen of bushes and a voice cried:

"Here, you get out of my car!"

"Oh, is it your car, Andy Foger?" asked Tom calmly as he recognized his squint-eyed rival. "I was just beginning to think it was. Allow me to return your wrench," and he held out the one he had picked up near the log. "The next time you drag trees across the road," went on the lad in the tonneau, facing the angry and dismayed Andy, "I'd advise you to post a notice at the top of the hill, so persons riding down will not be injured."

"Notice—road—hill—logs!" stammered Andy, turning red under his freckles.

"That's what I said," replied Tom coolly.

"I—I didn't have anything to do with putting a log across any road," mumbled the bully. "I—I've been off toward the creek."

"Have you?" asked Tom with a peculiar smile. "I thought you might have been looking for the wrench you dropped near the log. You should be more careful and so should Sam Snedecker, who's hiding outside the bushes," went on our hero, for he had caught sight of the form of Andy's crony

"I—I told him not to do it!" exclaimed Sam as he came from his hiding place.

"Shut up!" exclaimed Andy desperately.

"Oh, I think I know your secret," continued the young inventor. "You wanted to get even with me for outbidding you on the motor-boat. You watched which road I took, and then, in your auto, you came a shorter way, ahead of me. You hauled the log across the foot of the hill, hoping, I suppose, that my machine would be broken. But, let me tell you, it was a risky trick. Not only might I have been killed, but so would whoever else who happened to drive down the slope over the log, whether in a wagon or automobile. Fortunately Eradicate discovered it in time and warned me. I ought to have you arrested, but you're not worth it. A good thrashing is what such sneaks as you deserve!"

"You haven't got any evidence against us," sneered Andy confidently, his old bravado coming back.

"I have all I want," replied Tom. "You needn't worry. I'm not going to tell the police. But you've got to do one thing or I'll make you sorry you ever tried this trick. Eradicate will help me, so don't think you're going to escape."

"You get out of my automobile!" demanded Andy. "I'll have you arrested if you don't."

"I'll get out because I'm ready to, but not on account of your threats," retorted Mr. Swift's son. "Here's your wrench. Now I want you and Sam to start up this machine and haul that log out of the way."

"S'pose I won't do it?" snapped Andy.

"Then I'll cause your arrest, besides thrashing you into the bargain! You can take your choice of removing the log so travelers can pass or having a good hiding, you and Sam. Eradicate, you take Sam and I'll tackle Andy."

"Don't you dare touch me!" cried the bully, but there was a whine in his tones.

"You let me alone or I'll tell my father!" added Sam. "I—I didn't have nothin' to do with it, anyhow. I told Andy it would make trouble, but he made me help him."

"Say, what's the matter with you?" demanded Andy indignantly of his crony. "Do you want to——"

"I wish I'd never come with you," went on Sam, who was beginning to be frightened.

"Come now. Start up that machine and haul the log out of the way," demanded Tom again.

"I won't do it!" retorted the red-haired lad impudently.

"Yes, you will," insisted our hero, and he took a step toward the bully. They were out of the clump of bushes now and in the roadside ditch.

"You let me alone," almost screamed Andy, and in his baffled rage he rushed at Tom, aiming a blow.

The young inventor quickly stepped to one side, and, as the bully passed him, Tom sent out a neat left-hander. Andy Foger went down in a heap on the grass.

CHAPTER V

A TEST OF SPEED

WHETHER Tom or Andy was the most surprised at the happening would be hard to say. The former had not meant to hit so hard and he certainly did not intend to knock the squint-eyed youth down. The latter's fall was due, as much as anything, to his senseless, rushing tactics and to the fact that he slipped on the green grass. The bully was up in a moment, however, but he knew better than to try conclusions with Tom again. Instead he stood out of reach and splut-ʿred:

"You just wait, Tom Swift! You just wait!"

"Well, I'm waiting," responded the other calmly.

"I'll get even with you," went on Andy. "You think you're smart because you got ahead of me, but I'll get square!"

"Look here!" burst out the young inventor determinedly, taking a step toward his antagonist, at which Andy quickly retreated, "I don't want any more of that talk from you, Andy Foger. That's twice you've made threats against me to-day. You put that log across the road, and if you try anything like it for your second attempt I'll make you wish you hadn't. That applies to you, too, Sam," he added, glancing at the other lad.

"I—I ain't goin' to do nothin'," declared Sam. "I told Andy not to put that tree——"

"Keep still, can't you!' shouted the bully. "Come on. We'll get even with him, that's all," he muttered as he went back into the bushes where the auto was. Andy cranked up and he and his crony getting into the car were about to start off.

"Hold on!" cried Tom. "You'll take that log from across the road or I'll have you arrested for obstructing traffic, and that's a serious offense."

"I'm goin' to take it away!" growled Andy. "Give a fellow a show, can't you?"

He cast an ugly look at Tom, but the latter only smiled. It was no easy task for Sam and Andy to pull the log out of the way, as they could hardly lift it to slip the rope under. But they finally managed it, and, by the power of the car, hauled it to one side. Then they speed off.

"I 'clar t' gracious, dem young fellers am most as mean an' contrary as mah mule Boomerang am sometimes," observed Eradicate. "Only Boomerang ain't *quite* so mean as dat."

"I should hope not, Rad," observed Tom. "I'm ever so much obliged for your warning. I guess I'll be getting home now. Come around next week; we have some work for you."

" 'Deed an' I will," replied the colored man. "I'll come around an' eradicate all de dirt on yo' place, Mistah Swift. Yais, sah, I's Eradicate by name, and dat's my perfession—eradicatin' dirt. Much obleeged, I'll call around. Giddap, Boomerang !"

The mule lazily flicked his ears, but did not stir, and Tom, knowing that the process of arousing the animal would take some time, hurried up the hill to where he had left his motor-cycle. Eradicate was still engaged on the task of trying to arouse his steed to a sense of its duty when the young inventor flashed by on his way home.

"So you now own a broken motor-boat," observed Mr. Swift when Tom had related the circumstances of the auction. "Well, now you have it, what are you going to do with it?"

"Fix it, first of all," replied his son. "It needs considerable tinkering up, but nothing but what I can do, if you'll help me."

"Of course I will. Do you think you can get any speed out of it?"

"Well, I'm not so anxious for speed. I want a good, comfortable boat, and the *Arrow* will be that. I've named it, you see. I'm going back to Lanton this afternoon, take some tools along, and repair it so I can run the boat over to here. Then I'll get at it and fix it up. I've got a plan for you, dad."

"What is it?" asked the inventor, his rather tired face lighting up with interest.

"I'm going to take you on a vacation trip."

"A vacation trip?"

"Yes, you need a rest. You've been working too hard over that gyroscope invention."

"Yes, Tom, I think I have," admitted Mr. Swift. "But I am very much interested in it, and I think I can get it to work. If I do it will make a great difference in the control of aeroplanes. It will make them more stable and able to fly in almost any wind. But I certainly have puzzled my brains over some features of it. However, I don't quite see what you mean."

"You need a rest, dad," said Mr. Swift's son kindly. "I want you to forget all about patents, inventions, machinery and even the gyroscope for a week or two. When I get my motor-boat in shape I'm going to take you and Ned Newton up the lake for a cruise. We can camp out, or, if we had to, we could sleep in the boat. I'm going to put a canopy on it and arrange some bunks. It will do you good and perhaps new ideas for your gyroscope may come to you after a rest."

"Perhaps they will, Tom. I am certainly tired enough to need a vacation. It's very kind of you to think of me in connection with your boat. But if you're going to get it this afternoon you'd better start if you expect to get back by night. I think Mrs. Baggert has dinner ready."

After the meal Tom selected a number of tools from his own particular machine shop and carried them down to the dock on the lake, where his two small boats were tied.

"Aren't you going back on your motor-cycle?" asked his father.

"No, dad, I'm going to row over to Lanton, and, if I can get the *Arrow* fixed, I'll tow my rowboat back."

"Very well, then you won't be in any danger from Andy Foger. I must speak to his father about him."

"No, dad, don't," exclaimed the young inventor quickly. "I can fight my own battles with Andy. I don't fancy he will bother me again right away."

Tom found it more of a task than he had anticipated to get the motor in shape to run the *Arrow* back under her own power. The magneto was out of order and the batteries needed renewing, while the spark coil had short-circuited and took considerable time to adjust. But by using some new dry cells, which Mr. Hastings gave him, and cutting out the magneto, or small dynamo which produces the spark that exploded the gasoline in the cylinders, Tom soon had a fine, "fat" hot spark from the auxiliary ignition system. Then, adjusting the timer and throttle on the engine and seeing that the gasoline tank was filled, the lad started up his motor. Mr. Hastings helped him, but after a few turns of the fly-wheel there were no explosions. Finally, after the carburetor (which is the device where gasoline is mixed with air to produce an explosive mixture) had been adjusted, the motor started off as if it had intended to do so all the while and was only taking its time about it.

"The machine doesn't run as smooth as it ought to," commented Mr. Hastings.

"No, it needs a thorough overhauling," agreed the owner of the *Arrow*. "I'll get at it to-morrow," and with that he swung out into the lake, towing his rowboat after him.

"A motor-boat of my own!" exulted Tom as he twirled the steering-wheel and noted how readily the craft answered her helm. "This is great!"

He steered down the lake and then, turning around, went up it a mile or more before heading for his own dock, as he wanted to see how the engine behaved.

"With some changes and adjustments I can make this a speedy boat," thought Tom. "I'll get right at it. I shouldn't wonder if I could make a good showing against Mr. Hastings' new *Carlopa,* though his boat's got four cylinders and mine has but two."

The lad was proceeding leisurely along the lake shore, near his home, with the motor throttled down to test it at low speed, when he heard some one shout. Looking toward the bank, Tom saw a man waving his hands.

"I wonder what he wants?" thought our hero as he put the wheel over to send his craft to shore. He heard a moment later, for the man on the bank cried:

"I say, my young friend, do you know anything about automobiles? Of course you do or you wouldn't be running a motor-boat. Bless my very existence, but I'm in trouble! My machine has stopped on a lonely road and I can't seem to get it started. I happened to hear your boat and I came here to hail you. Bless my coat-pockets but I am in trouble! Can you help me? Bless my soul and gizzard!"

"Mr. Damon," exclaimed Tom, shutting off the power, for he was now near shore. "Of course

I'll help you, Mr. Damon," for the young inventor
had recognized the eccentric man of whom he had
purchased the motor-cycle and who had helped
him in rounding up the thieves.

"Why, bless my shoe-laces, if it isn't Tom
Swift!" exclaimed Mr. Damon, who seemed very
fond of calling down blessings upon himself or
upon articles of his dress or person.

"Yes, I'm here," admitted Tom with a laugh.

"And in a motor-boat, too! Bless my pocket-
book, but did that run away with some one who
sold it to you cheap?"

"No, not exactly," and the lad explained how
he had come into possession of it. By this time
he was ashore and had tied the *Arrow* to an overhanging tree. Then Tom proceeded to where Mr.
Damon had left his stalled automobile. The eccentric man was wealthy and his physician had
instructed him to ride about in the car for his
health. Tom soon located the trouble. The carburetor had become clogged, and it was soon in
working order again.

"Well, now that you have a boat, I don't suppose you will be riding about the country so
much," commented Mr. Damon as he got into his
car. "Bless my spark-plug! but if you ever get
over to Waterfield, where I live, come and see me.
It's handy to get to by water."

"I'll come some day," promised the lad.

"Bless my hat band, but I hope so," went on the eccentric individual as he prepared to start his car.

Tom completed the remainder of the trip to his boathouse without incident and his father came down to the dock to see the motor-boat. He agreed with his son that it was a bargain and that it could easily be put in fine shape.

The youth spent all the next day and part of the following working on the craft. He overhauled the ignition system, which was the jump-spark style, cleaned the magneto and adjusted the gasoline and compression taps so that they fitted better. Then he readjusted the rudder lines, tightening them on the steering-wheel, and looked over the piping from the gasoline tank.

The tank was in the forward compartment, and, upon inspecting this, the lad concluded to change the plan by which the big galvanized iron box was held in place. He took out the old wooden braces and set them closer together, putting in a few new ones.

"The tank will not vibrate so when I'm going at full speed," he explained to his father.

"Is that where the strange man was tampering with the lock the day of the auction?" asked Mr. Swift.

"Yes, but I don't see what he could want in this compartment, do you, dad?"

The inventor got into the boat and looked carefully into the rather dark space where the tank fitted. He went over every inch of it, and, pointing to one of the thick wooden blocks that supported the tank, asked:

"Did you bore that hole in there, Tom?"

"No, it was there before I touched the braces. But it isn't a hole, or, rather, some one bored it and stopped it up again. It doesn't weaken the brace any."

"No, I suppose not. I was just wondering whether that was one of the new blocks or an old one."

"Oh, an old one. I'm going to paint them, too, so in case the water leaks in or the gasoline leaks out the wood won't be affected. A gasoline tank should vibrate as little as possible, if you don't want it to leak. I guess I'll paint the whole interior of this compartment white, then I can see away into the far corners of it."

"I think that's a good idea," commented Mr. Swift.

It was four days after his purchase of the boat before Tom was ready to make a long trip in it. Up to that time he had gone on short spins not far from the dock, in order to test the engine adjustment. The lad found it was working very well, but he decided with a new kind of spark plugs for the two cylinders that he could get more speed out of it. Finally the forward compartment was painted, a general overhauling given the hull and Tom was ready to put his boat to a good test.

"Come on, Ned," he said to his chum early one evening after Mr. Swift had said he was too tired to go out on a trial run. "We'll see what the *Arrow* will do now."

From the time Tom started up the motor it was evident that the boat was going through the water at a rapid rate. For a mile or more the two lads speeded along, enjoying it hugely. Then Ned exclaimed:

"Something's coming behind us."

Tom turned his head and looked. Then he called out:

"It's Mr. Hastings in his new *Carlopa*. I wonder if he wants a race?"

"Guess he'd have it all his own way," suggested Ned.

"Oh, I don't know. I can get a little more speed out of my boat."

Tom waited until the former owner of the *Arrow* was up to him.

"Want a race?" asked Mr. Hastings good-naturedly.

"Sure!" agreed Tom, and he shoved the timer ahead to produce quicker explosions.

The *Arrow* seemed to leap forward and for a moment was ahead of the *Carlopa,* but with a motion of his hand to the spark lever Mr. Hastings also increased his speed. For a moment the two boats were on even terms and then the larger and newer one forged ahead. Tom had expected it, but he was a little disappointed.

"That's doing first rate," complimented Mr. Hastings as he passed them. "Better than I was ever able to make her do even when she was new, Tom."

This made the present owner of the *Arrow* feel somewhat consoled. He and Ned ran on for a few miles, the *Carlopa* in the meanwhile disappearing from view around a bend. Then Tom and his chum turned around and made for the Swift dock.

"She certainly is a dandy!" declared Ned. "I wish I had one like it."

"Oh, I intend that you shall have plenty of rides in this," went on his friend. "When you get your vacation, you and dad and I are going on a tour," and he explained his plan, which, it is needless to say, met with Ned's hearty approval.

Just before going to bed, some hours later, Tom decided to go down to the dock to make sure he had shut off the gasoline cock leading from the tank of his boat to the motor. It was a calm, early summer night, with a new moon giving a little light, and the lad went down to the lake in his slippers. As he neared the boathouse he heard a noise.

"Water rat," he murmured, "or maybe musk-rats. I must set some traps."

As Tom entered the boathouse he started back in alarm, for a bright light flashed up, almost in his eyes.

"Who's here?" he cried, and at that moment some one sprang out of his motor-boat, scrambled into a rowing craft which the youth could dimly make out in front of the dock and began to pull away quickly.

"Hold on there!" cried the young inventor. "Who are you? What do you want? Come back here!"

The person in the boat returned no answer. With his heart doing beats over-time Tom lighted a lantern and made a hasty examination of the *Arrow.* It did not appear to have been harmed, but a glance showed that the door of the gasoline compartment had been unlocked and was open. Tom jumped down into his craft.

"Some one has been at that compartment again!" he murmured. "I wonder if it was the same man who acted so suspiciously at the auction? What can his object be, anyhow?"

The next moment he uttered an exclamation of startled surprise and picked up something from the bottom of the boat. It was a bunch of keys, with a tag attached, bearing the owner's name.

"Andy Foger!" murmured Tom. "So this is how he was trying to get even! Maybe he started to put a hole in the tank or in my boat."

CHAPTER VI

TOWING SOME GIRLS

WITH a sense of anger mingled with an apprehension lest some harm should have been done to his craft, the owner of the *Arrow* went carefully over it. He could find nothing wrong. The engine was all right and all that appeared to have been accomplished by the unbidden visitor was the opening of the locked forward compartment. That this had been done by one of the many keys on Andy Foger's ring was evident.

"Now what could have been his object?" mused Tom. "I should think if he wanted to put a hole in the boat he would have done it amidships, where the water would have a better chance to come in, or perhaps he wanted to flood it with gasoline and——"

The idea of fire was in Tom's mind, and he did not finish his half-completed thought.

"That may have been it," he resumed after a hasty examination of the gasoline tank, to make sure there were no leaks in it. "To get even with

me for outbidding him on the boat, Andy may
have wanted to destroy the *Arrow*. Well, of all
the mean tricks, that's about the limit! But wait
until I see him. I've got evidence against him,"
and Tom looked at the key ring. "I could almost
have him arrested for this."

Going outside the boathouse, Tom stood on the
edge of the dock and peered into the darkness.
He could hear the faint sound of some one rowing across the lake, but there was no light.

"He had one of those electric flash lanterns,"
decided Tom. "If I hadn't found his keys, I
might have thought it was Happy Harry instead
of Andy.

The young inventor went back into the house
after carefully locking the boat compartment and
detaching from the engine an electrical device,
without which the motor in the *Arrow* could not
be started.

"That will prevent them from running away
with my boat, anyhow," decided Tom. "And I'll
tell Garret Jackson to keep a sharp watch to-
night." Jackson was the engineer at Mr. Swift's
workshop.

Tom told his father of the happening and Mr.
Swift was properly indignant. He wanted to go
at once to see Mr. Foger and complain of Andy's
act, but Tom counseled waiting.

"I'll attend to Andy myself," said the young inventor. "He's getting desperate, I guess, or he wouldn't try to set the place on fire. But wait until I show him these keys."

Bright and early the next morning the owner of the motor-boat was down to the dock inspecting it. The engineer, who had been on watch part of the night, reported that there had been no disturbance, and Tom found everything all right.

"I wonder if I'd better go over and accuse Andy now or wait until I see him and spring this evidence on him?" thought our hero. Then he decided it would be better to wait. He took the *Arrow* out after breakfast, his father going on a short spin with him.

"But I must go back now and work on my gyroscope invention," said Mr. Swift when about two hours had been spent on the lake. "I am making good progress with it."

"You need a vacation," decided Tom. "I'll be ready to take you and Ned in about two weeks. He will have two weeks off then and we'll have some glorious times together."

That afternoon Tom put some new style spark plugs in the cylinders of his motor and found that he had considerably increased the revolutions of the engine, due to a better explosion being obtained. He also made some minor adjustments and the next day he went out alone for a long run.

Heading up the lake, Tom was soon in sight of a popular excursion resort that was frequently visited by church and Sunday-school organizations in the vicinity of Shopton. The lad saw a number of rowing craft and a small motor-boat circling around opposite the resort and remarked:

"There must be a picnic at the grove to-day. Guess I'll run up and take a look."

The lad was soon in the midst of quite a flotilla of rowboats, most of them manned by pretty girls or in charge of boys who were giving sisters (their own or some other chap's) a trip on the water. Tom throttled his boat down to slow speed and looked with pleasure on the pretty scene. His boat attracted considerable attention, for motor craft were not numerous on Lake Carlopa.

As our hero passed a boat, containing three very pretty young ladies, Tom heard one of them exclaim:

"There he is now! That's Tom Swift."

Something in the tones of the voice attracted his attention. He turned and saw a brown-eyed girl smiling at him. She bowed and asked, blushing the while:

"Well, have you caught any more runaway horses lately?"

"Runaway horses—why—what? Oh, it's Miss Nestor!" exclaimed the lad, recognizing the young lady whose steed he had frightened one day when he was on his bicycle. As told in the first volume of this series, the horse had run away, being alarmed at the flashing of Tom's wheel, and Miss Mary Nestor, of Mansburg, was in grave danger.

"So you've given up the bicycle for the motor-boat," went on the young lady.

"Yes," replied Tom with a smile, shutting off the power, "and I haven't had a chance to save any girls since I've had it."

The two boats had drifted close together, and Miss Nestor introduced her two companions to Tom.

"Don't you want to come in and take a ride?" he asked.

"Is it safe?" asked Jennie Haddon, one of the trio.

"Of course it is, Jennie, or he wouldn't be out in it," said Miss Nestor hastily. "Come on, let's get in. I'm just dying for a motor-boat ride."

"What will we do with our boat?" asked Katie Carson.

"Oh, I can tow that," replied the youth. "Get right in and I'll take you all around the lake."

"Not too far," stipulated the girl who had figured in the runaway. "We must be back for lunch, which will be served in about an hour. Our church and Sunday-school are having a picnic."

"Maybe Mr. Swift will come and have some lunch with us," suggested Miss Carson, blushing prettily.

"Nothing would give me greater pleasure," answered Tom, and then he laughed at his formal reply, the girls joining in.

"We'd be glad to have you," added Miss Haddon. "Oh!" she suddenly screamed, "the boat's tipping over!"

"Oh, no," Tom hastened to assure her, coming to the side to help her in. "It just tilts a bit, with the weight of so many on one side. It couldn't capsize if it tried."

In another moment the three were in the roomy cockpit and Tom had made the empty rowboat fast to the stern. He was about to start up when from another boat, containing two little girls and two slightly larger boys, came a plaintive cry:

"Oh, mister, give us a ride!"

"Sure!" agreed Tom pleasantly. "Just fasten your boat to the other rowboat and I'll tow you."

One of the boys did this, and then, with three pretty girls as his companions in the *Arrow* and towing the two boats, Tom started off.

The girls were very much interested in the craft

and asked all sorts of questions about how the
engine operated. Tom explained as clearly as he
could how the gasoline exploded in the cylinders,
about the electric spark and about the propeller.
Then, when he had finished, Miss Haddon remarked naively:

"Oh, Mr. Swift, you've explained it beautifully, and I'm sure if our teacher in school made
things as clear as you have that I could get along
fine. I understand all about it, except I don't see
what makes the engine go."

"Oh," said Tom faintly, and he wondering
what would be the best remark to make under the
circumstances, when Miss Nestor created a diversion by looking at her watch and exclaiming:

"Oh, girls, it's lunch time! We must go
ashore. Will you kindly put about, Mr. Swift—I
hope that is the proper term—and—land us—is
that right?" and she looked archly at Tom.

"That's perfectly right," he admitted with a
laugh and a glance into the girl's brown eyes.
"I'll put you ashore at once," and he headed for a
small dock.

"And come yourself to take lunch with us,"
added Miss Haddon.

"I'm afraid I might be in the way," stammered
Tom. "I—I have a pretty good appetite,
and——"

"I suppose you think that girls on a picnic don't take much lunch," finished Miss Nestor. "But I assure you that we have plenty, and that you will be very welcome," she added warmly.

"Yes, and I'd like to have him explain over again how the engine works," went on Miss Haddon. "I am *so* interested."

Tom helped the girls out, receiving their thanks as well as those of the children in the second boat. But as he walked with the young ladies through the grove the young inventor registered a mental vow that he would steer clear of explaining again how a gasoline engine worked.

"Now come right over this way to our table," invited Miss Nestor. "I want you to meet papa and mamma."

Tom followed her. As he stepped from behind a clump of trees he saw, standing not far away, a figure that seemed strangely familiar. A moment later the figure turned and Tom saw Andy Foger confronting him. At the sight of our hero the bully turned red and walked quickly away, while Tom's fingers touched the ring of keys in his pocket.

CHAPTER VII

A BRUSH WITH ANDY

So UNEXPECTED was his encounter with Andy
that the young inventor hardly knew how to act,
especially since he was a guest of the young ladies.
Tom did not want to do or say anything to em-
barrass them or make a scene, yet he did want to
have a talk, and a very serious talk, with Andy
Foger.

Miss Nestor must have noticed Tom's sudden
start at his glimpse of Andy, for she asked:

"Did you see some one you knew, Mr. Swift?"

"Yes," replied Tom, "I did—er—that is——"
He paused in some confusion.

"Perhaps you'd like—that is prefer—to go with
them instead of taking lunch with girls who don't
know anything about engines?" she persisted.

"Oh, no indeed," Tom hastened to assure her.
"He—that is—the person I saw wouldn't care to
have me lunch with him," and the youth smiled
grimly.

"Would you like to bring him over to our table?" inquired Miss Carson. "We have plenty for him."

"No, I think that would hardly do," continued the lad, who tried not to smile at the picture of the red-haired and squint-eyed Andy Foger making one of a party with the girls. The young ladies fortunately had not noticed the bully, who was out of view by this time.

Tom was presented to Mr. and Mrs. Nestor, who told him how glad they were to meet the young man who had been instrumental in saving their daughter from injury, if not death. Tom was a bit embarrassed, but bore the praise as well as he could, and he was very glad when a diversion, in the shape of lunch, occurred.

After a meal on tables under the trees in the grove Tom took the girls and some of their friends out in his motor-boat again. They covered several miles around the lake before returning to the picnic ground.

As Tom was starting toward home in his boat, wondering what had become of Andy and trying to think of a reason why the bully should attend anything as "tame" as a church picnic, the object of his thoughts came strolling through the trees down to the shore of the lake. The moment he saw Tom the red-haired lad started back, but the young inventor, leaping out of his boat, called out:

"Hold on there, Andy Foger, I want to see you!" and there was menace in Tom's tone.

"But I don't want to see you!" retorted the other sulkily. "I've got no use for you."

"No more have I for you," was Tom's quick reply. "But I want to return you these keys. You dropped them in my boat the other night when you tried to set it afire. If I ever catch you——"

"My keys! Your boat! On fire!" gasped Andy, so plainly astonished that Tom knew his surprise was genuine.

"Yes, your keys. You were a little too quick for me or I'd have caught you at it. The next time you pick a lock don't leave your keys behind you," and he held out the jingling ring.

Andy Foger advanced slowly. He took the bunch of keys and looked at the tag.

"They *are* mine," he said slowly, as if there was some doubt about it.

"Of course they are," declared Tom. "I found them where you dropped them—in my boat."

"Do you mean over at the auction?"

"No, I mean down in my boathouse, where you sneaked in the other night and tried to do some damage."

"The other night!" cried Andy. "I never was near your boathouse any night and I never lost my keys there! I lost these the day of the auction, on Mr. Hastings' ground, and I've been looking for them ever since."

"Didn't you sneak in my boathouse the other night and try to do some mischief? Didn't you drop them then?"

"No, I didn't," retorted Andy earnestly. "I lost those keys at the auction, and I can prove it to you. Look, I advertised for them in the weekly *Gazette*."

The red-haired lad pulled a crumpled paper from his pocket and showed Tom an advertisement offering a reward of two dollars for a bunch of keys on a ring, supposed to have been lost at the auction on Mr. Hastings' grounds in Lanton. The finder was to return them to Andy Foger.

"Does that look as if I lost the keys in your boathouse?" demanded the bully sneeringly. "I wouldn't have advertised them that way if I'd been trying to keep my visit quiet. Besides, I can prove that I was out of town several nights. I was over to an entertainment in Mansburg one night and I didn't get home until two o'clock in the morning, because my machine broke down. Ask Ned Newton. He saw me at the entertainment."

Andy's manner was so earnest that Tom could not help believing him. Then there was the evidence of the advertisement. Clearly the squint-eyed youth had not been the mysterious visitor to the boathouse and had not unlocked the forward compartment. But if it was not he, who could it have been and how did the keys get there? These were questions which racked Tom's brain.

"You can ask Ned Newton," repeated Andy. "He'll prove that I couldn't have been near your place, if you don't believe me."

"Oh, I believe you all right," answered Tom, for there could be no doubting Andy's manner, even though he and the young inventor were not on good terms. "But how did your keys get in my boat?"

"I don't know, unless you found them, kept them and dropped them there," was the insolent answer.

"You know better than that," exclaimed Tom.

"Well, I owe you a reward of two dollars for giving them back to me," continued the bully patronizingly. "Here it is," and he hauled out some bills.

"I don't want your money!" fired back Tom. "But I'd like to know who it was that was in my boat."

"And I'd like to know who it was took my

keys," and Andy stuffed the money back in his pocket. Tom did not answer. He was puzzling over a queer matter and he wanted to be alone and think. He turned aside from the red-haired lad and walked toward his motor-boat.

"I'll give you a surprise in a few days," Andy called after him, but Tom did not turn his head nor did he inquire what the surprise might be.

Mr. Swift was somewhat puzzled when his son related the outcome of the key incident. He agreed with Tom that some one might have found the ring and kept it, and that the same person might have been the one whom Tom had surprised in the boathouse.

"But it's idle to speculate on it," commented the inventor. "Andy might have induced some of his chums to act for him in harming your boat, and the key advertisement might have been only a ruse."

"I hardly think so," answered his son, shaking his head. "It strikes me as being very curious, and I'm going to see if I can't get at the bottom of it."

But a week or more passed and Tom had nc clew. In the meanwhile he was working away at his motor-boat, installing several improvements.

One of these was a better pump, which circulated the water around the cylinders, and another was a new system of lubrication under forced feed.

"This ought to give me a little more speed," reasoned Tom, who was not yet satisfied with his craft. "Guess I'll take it out for a spin."

He was alone in the *Arrow,* taking a long course up the lake when, as he passed a wooded point that concealed from view a sort of bay, he heard the puffing of another motor-boat.

"Maybe that's Mr. Hastings," thought Tom. "If I raced with him now, I think the *Arrow* could give a better account of herself.

The young inventor looked at the boat as it came into view. It needed but a glance to show that it was not the *Carlopa.* Then, as it came nearer, Tom saw a familiar figure in it—a red-haired, squint-eyed chap.

"Andy Foger!" exclaimed Tom. "He's got a motor-boat! This is the surprise he spoke of."

The boat was rapidly approaching him, and he saw that it was painted a vivid red. Then he could make out the name on the bow, *Red Streak.* Andy was sending the craft toward him at a fast rate.

"You needn't think you're the only one on this lake who has a gasoline boat!" called Andy boastfully. "This is my new one and the fastest thing

afloat around here. I can go all around you. Do
you want to race?"

It was a "dare," and Tom never took such
things when he could reasonably enter a contest.
He swung his boat around so as to shoot alongside of Andy and answered:

"Yes, I'll race you. Where to?"

"Down opposite Kolb's dock and back to this
point," was the answer. "I'll give you a start, as
my engine has three cylinders. This is a racing
boat."

"I don't need any start," declared Tom. "I'll
race you on even terms. Go ahead!"

Both lads adjusted their timers to get more
speed. The water began to curl away from the
sharp prows, the motors exploded faster and
faster. The race was on between the *Arrow* and
the *Red Streak*.

CHAPTER VIII

OFF ON A TRIP

GLANCING with critical eyes at the craft of his rival, Tom saw that Andy Foger had a very fine boat. The young inventor also realized that if he was to come anywhere near winning the race he would have to get the utmost speed out of his engine, for the new boat the bully had was designed primarily for racing, while Tom's was an all-around pleasure craft, though capable of something in the speed line.

"I'll be giving you a tow in a few minutes, as soon as my engine gets warmed up!" sneered Andy.

"Maybe," said Tom, and then he crouched down to make as little resistance as possible to the wind. Andy, on the contrary, sat boldly upright at the auto steering-wheel of his boat.

On rushed the two motor craft, their prows exactly even and the propellers tossing up a bulge in the water at their sterns. Rapidly acquiring speed after the two lads had adjusted the timers on their motors, the boats were racing side by side, seemingly on even terms.

The *Red Streak* had a very sharp prow, designed to cut through the water. It was of the type known as an automobile launch. That is, the engine was located forward, under a sort of hood, which had two hinged covers like a bat's wings. The steering-wheel shaft went through the forward bulkhead, slantingly, like the wheel of an auto, and was arranged with gasoline and sparking levers on the center post in a similar manner. At the right of the wheel was a reversing lever, by which the propeller blades could be set at neutral, or arranged so as to drive the boat backward. Altogether the *Red Streak* was a very fine boat and had cost considerably more than had Tom's, even when the latter was new. All these things the young owner of the *Arrow* thought of as he steered his craft over the course.

"I hardly think I can win," Tom remarked to himself in a whisper. "His boat is too speedy for this one. I have a chance, though, for his engine is new, and I don't believe he understands it as well as I do mine. Then, too, I am sure I have a better ignition system."

But if Tom had any immediate hopes of defeating Andy, they were doomed to disappointment, for about two minutes after the race started the *Red Streak* forged slowly ahead.

"Come on!" cried the red-haired lad. "I thought you wanted a race."

"I do," answered the young inventor. "We're a long way from the dock yet, and we've got to come back."

"You'll be out of it by the time I get to the dock," declared Andy.

Indeed it began to look so, for the auto boat was now a full length ahead of Tom's craft and there was open water between them. But our hero knew a thing or two about racing, though he had not long been a motor-boat owner. He adjusted the automatic oiler on the cylinders to give more lubrication, as he intended to get more speed out of his engine. Then he opened the gasoline cock a trifle more and set his timer forward a few notches to get an earlier spark. He was not going to use the maximum speed just yet, but he first wanted to see how the motor of the *Arrow* would behave under these conditions. To his delight he saw his boat slowly creeping up on Andy's. The latter, with a glance over his shoulder, saw it too, and he advanced his spark. His craft forged ahead, but the rate of increase was not equal to Tom's.

"If I can keep up to him I suppose I ought to

be glad," thought the young inventor, "for his boat is away ahead of mine in rating."

Through the water the sharp bows cut. There were only a few witnesses to the race, but those who were out in boats saw a pretty sight as the two speedy craft came on toward the dock, which was the turning point.

Andy's boat reached it first, and swung about in a wide circle for the return. Tom decided it was time to make his boat do its best, so he set the timer at the limit, and the spark, coming more quickly, increased the explosions.

Up shot the *Arrow* and, straightening out after the turn, Tom's craft crept along until it lapped the stern of the *Red Streak*. Andy looked back in dismay. Then he tried to get more speed out of his engine. He did cause the screw to revolve a little faster, and Tom noted that he was again being left behind. Then one of those things which may happen at any time to a gasoline motor happened to Andy's. It began to miss explosions. At first it was only occasionally, then the misses became more frequent.

The owner of the *Red Streak* with one hand on the steering-wheel, tried with the other to adjust the motor to get rid of the trouble, but he only made it worse. Andy's boat began to fall back and Tom's to creep up. Frantically Andy worked the gasoline and sparking levers, but without avail. At last one cylinder went completely out of service.

The two boats were now on even terms and were racing along side by side toward the wooded point, which marked the finish.

"I'll beat you yet!" exclaimed Andy fiercely.

"Better hurry up!" retorted Tom.

But the young inventor was not to have it all his own way. With a freakishness equal to that with which it had ceased to explode the dead cylinder came to life again, and the *Red Streak* shot ahead. Once more Andy's boat had the lead of a length and the finish of the race was close at hand. The squint-eyed lad turned and shouted:

"I told you I'd beat you! Want a tow now?"

It began to look as though Tom would need it, but he still had something in reserve. One of the improvements he had put in the *Arrow* was a new auxiliary ignition system. This he now decided to use.

With a quick motion Tom threw over the switch that put it into operation. A hotter, "fatter" spark was at once produced, and adjusting his gasoline cock so that a little more of the fluid would be drawn in, making a "richer" mixture, the owner of the *Arrow* saw the craft shoot forward as if, like some weary runner, new life had been infused.

In vain did Andy frantically try to get more speed out of his motor. He cut out the muffler, and the explosions sounded loudly over the lake. But it was no use. A minute later the *Arrow*, which had slowly forged ahead, crossed the bows of the *Red Streak* opposite the finishing point, and Tom had won the race.

"Well, was that fair?" our hero called to Andy, who had quickly shut off some of his power as he saw his rival's daring trick. "Did I beat you fair?"

"You wouldn't have beaten me if my engine hadn't gone back on me," grumbled Andy, chagrin showing on his face. "Wait until my motor runs smoother and I'll give you a big handicap and beat you. My boat's faster than yours. It ought to be. It cost fifteen hundred dollars and it's a racer."

"I guess it doesn't like racing," commented Tom as he swung the prow of his craft down the lake toward his home. But he knew there was some truth in what Andy had said. The *Red Streak* was a more speedy boat, and, with proper handling, could have beaten the *Arrow*. That was where Tom's superior knowledge came in useful.

"Just you wait, I'll beat you yet," called Andy

after the young inventor, but the latter made no answer. He was satisfied.

Mr. Swift was much interested that night in his son's account of the race.

"I had no idea yours was such a speedy boat," he said.

"Well, it wasn't originally," admitted Tom, "but the improvements I put on it made it so. But, dad, when are we going on our tour? You look more worn out than I've seen you in some time, not excepting when the turbine model was stolen. Are you worrying over your gyroscope invention?"

"Somewhat, Tom. I can't seem to hit on just what I want. It's a difficult problem."

"Then I tell you what let's do, dad. Let's drop everything in the inventive line and go off on a vacation. I'll take you up the lake in my boat and you can spend a week at the Lakeview Hotel at Sandport. It will do you good."

"What will you do, Tom?"

"Oh, Ned Newton and I will cruise about and we'll take you along any time you want to go. We're going to camp out nights or sleep in the boat if it rains. I've ordered a canopy with side curtains. Ned and I don't care for the hotel life in the summer. Will you go?"

Mr. Swift considered a moment. He did need

a rest, for he had been working hard and his brain was weary with thinking of many problems. His son's program sounded very attractive.

"I think I will accept," said the inventor with a smile. "When can you start, Tom?"

"In about four days. Ned Newton will get his vacation then and I'll have the canopy on. I'll start to work at it to-morrow. Then we'll go on a trip."

Sandport was a summer resort at the extreme southern end of Lake Carlopa, and Mr. Swift at once wrote to the Lakeview Hotel there to engage a room for himself. In the meanwhile Tom began to put the canopy on his boat and arrange for the trip, which would take nearly a whole day. Ned Newton was delighted with the prospect of a camping tour and helped Tom to get ready. They took a small tent and plenty of supplies, with some food. They did not need to carry many rations, as the shores of the lake were lined with towns and villages where food could be procured.

Finally all was ready for the trip and the night before the start Ned Newton stayed at Tom's house so as to be in readiness for going off early in the morning. The day was all that could be desired, Tom noted, as he and his chum hurried down to the dock before breakfast to put their blankets in the boat. As the young inventor entered the craft he uttered an exclamation.

"What's the matter?" asked Ned.

"I was sure I locked the sliding door of that forward compartment," was the reply. "Now it's open." He looked inside the space occupied by the gasoline tank and cried out: "One of the braces is gone! There's been some one at my boat in the night and they tried to damage her."

"Much harm done?" 'asked Ned anxiously.

"No, none at all, to speak of," replied Tom. "I can easily put a new block under the tank. In fact, I don't really need all I have. But why should any one take one out, and who did it? That's what I want to know."

The two lads looked carefully about the dock and boat for a sign of the missing block or any clews that might show who had been tampering with the *Arrow*, but they could find nothing.

"Maybe the block fell out," suggested Ned.

"It couldn't," replied Tom. "It was one of the new ones I put in myself and it was nailed fast. You can see where it's been pried loose. I can't understand it," and Tom thought rapidly of several mysterious occurrences of late in which the strange man at the auction and the person he had surprised one night in the boathouse had a part.

"Well, it needn't delay our trip," resumed the

young inventor. "Maybe there's a hoodoo around here, and it will do us good to get away a few days. Come on, we'll have breakfast, get dad and start."

A little later the *Arrow* was puffing away up the lake in the direction of Sandport.

CHAPTER IX

MR. SWIFT IS ALARMED

"Don't you feel better already, dad?" asked Tom that noon as they stopped under a leaning, overhanging tree for lunch on the shore of the lake. "I'll leave it to Ned if you don't look more contented and less worried."

"I believe he does," agreed the other lad.

"Well, I must say I certainly have enjoyed the outing so far," admitted the inventor with a smile. "And I haven't been bothering about my gyroscope. I think I'll take another sandwich, Tom, and a few more olives."

"That's the way to talk!" cried the son. "Your appetite is improving, too. If Mrs. Baggert could see you she'd say so."

"Oh, yes, Mrs. Baggert. I do hope she and Garret will look after the house and shops well," said Mr. Swift, and the old, worried look came like a shadow over his face.

"Now don't be thinking of that, dad," advised

Tom. "Of course everything will be all right. Do you think some of those model thieves will return and try to get some of your other inventions?"

"I don't know, Tom. Those men were unscrupulous scoundrels, and you can never tell what they might do to revenge themselves on us for defeating their plans."

"Well, I guess Garret and Mrs. Baggert will look out for them," remarked his son. "Don't worry."

"Yes, it's bad for the digestion," added Ned. "If you don't mind, Tom, I'll have some more coffee and another sandwich myself."

"Nothing the matter with your appetite, either," commented the young inventor as he passed the coffee pot and the plate.

They were soon on their way again, the *Arrow* making good time up the lake. Tom was at the engine, making several minor adjustments to it, while Ned steered. Mr. Swift reclined on one of the cushioned seats under the shade of the canopy. The young owner of the *Arrow* looked over the stretch of water from time to time for a possible sight of Andy Foger, but the *Red Streak* was not to be seen. The Lakeview Hotel was reached late that afternoon and the boat was tied up to the

dock, while Tom and Ned accompanied Mr. Swift
to see him comfortably established in his room.

"Won't you stay to supper with me?" invited
the inventor to his son and the latter's chum. "Or
do you want to start right in on camp life?"

"I guess we'll stay to supper and remain at the
hotel to-night," decided Tom. "We got here a
little later than I expected, and Ned and I hardly
have time to go very far and establish a temporary
camp. We'll live a life of luxurious ease to-night
and begin to be 'wanderlusters' and get back to
nature to-morrow."

In the morning Tom and his chum, full of enthusiasm for the pleasures before them, started
off, promising to come back to the hotel in a few
days to see how Mr. Swift felt. The trip had
already done the man good and his face wore a
brighter look.

Tom and Ned, in the speedy *Arrow*, cruised
along the lake shores all that morning. At noon
they went ashore, made a temporary camp and
arranged to spend the night there in the tent.
After this was erected they got out their fishing
tackle and passed the afternoon at that sport, having such good luck that they provided their own
supper without having to depend on canned stuff.

They lived this life for three days, making a
new camp each night, being favored with good

weather, so that they did not have to sleep in the boat to keep dry. On the afternoon of the third day Tom, with a critical glance at the sky, remarked:

"I shouldn't be surprised if it rained to-morrow, Ned."

"Me either. It does look sort of hazy, and the wind is in a bad quarter."

"Then what do you say to heading for the hotel? I fancy dad will be glad to see us."

"That suits me. We can start camp life again after the storm passes."

They started for Sandport that afternoon. When within about two miles of the hotel dock Tom saw, just ahead of them, a small motor-boat. Ned observed it too and called out:

"S'pose that's Andy looking for another race?"

"No, the boat's too small for his. We'll put over that way and see who it is."

The other craft did not appear to be moving very rapidly and the *Arrow* was soon overhauling it. As the two chums came nearer they could hear the puffing of the motor. Tom listened with critical ears.

"That machine isn't working right," he remarked to his chum.

At that moment there sounded a loud explosion

from the other boat and at the same time there came over the water a shrill cry of alarm.

"That's a girl in that boat!" exclaimed Ned. "Maybe she's hurt."

"No, the motor only back-fired," observed Tom. "But we'll go over and see if we can help her. Perhaps she doesn't understand it. Girls don't know much about machinery."

A little later the *Arrow* shot up alongside the other craft, which had come to a stop. The two lads could see a girl bending over the motor, twirling the fly-wheel and trying to get it started.

"Can I help you?" asked Tom, shutting off the power from his craft.

The young lady glanced up. Her face was red and she seemed ill at ease. At the sight of the young inventor she uttered an exclamation of relief.

"Why, Mr. Swift!" she cried. "Oh, I'm in such trouble. I can't make the machine work, and I'm afraid it's broken; it exploded."

"Miss Nestor!" blurted out Tom, more surprised evidently to see his acquaintance of the runaway again than she was at beholding him. "I didn't know you ran a motor-boat," he added.

"I don't," said she simply and helplessly. "That's the trouble, it won't run."

"How comes it that you are up here?" went on Tom.

"I am stopping with friends, who have a cottage near the Lakeview Hotel. They have a motor-boat and I got Dick Blythe—he's the owner of this—to show me how to run it. I thought I knew, and I started out a little while ago. At first it went beautifully, but a few minutes ago it blew up, or—or something dreadful happened."

"Nothing very dreadful, I guess," Tom assured her. "I think I can fix it." He got into the other boat and soon saw what the trouble was. The carburetor had gotten out of adjustment and the gasoline was not feeding properly. The young inventor soon had it in order, and, testing the motor, found that it worked perfectly.

"Oh, I can't thank you enough," cried Miss Nestor with a flash from her brown eyes that made Tom's heart beat double time. "I was afraid I had damaged the boat, and I knew Dick, who is a sort of second cousin of mine, would never forgive me."

"There's no harm done," Tom assured her. "But you had better keep near us on your way back; that is, if you are going back."

"Oh, indeed I am. I was frightened when I found I'd come so far away from shore, and then, when that explosion took place—well, you can imagine how I felt. Indeed I will keep near you. Are you stopping near here? If you are, I wish you'd come and see me, you and Mr. Newton," she added, for Tom had introduced his chum.

"I'll be very glad to," answered our hero, and he told how he happened to be in the neighborhood. "I'll give you a few lessons in managing a boat, if you like," he added.

"Oh, will you? That will be lovely! I won't tell Dick about it, and I'll surprise him some day by showing him how well I can run his boat."

"Good idea," commented Tom.

He started the motor for Miss Nestor, having stopped it after his first test, and then, with the *Dot*, which was the name of the small boat Miss Nestor was in, following the larger *Arrow*, the run back to the hotel was made. The young lady turned off near the Lakeview dock to go to the cottage where she was stopping and the lads tied up at the hotel boathouse.

"Yes, we are in for a storm," remarked Tom as he and his chum walked up toward the hotel. "I wonder how dad is? I hope the outing is doing him good."

"There he comes now," observed Ned, and, looking up, Tom saw his father approaching. The young inventor was at once struck by the expression on his parent's face. Mr. Swift looked worried and Tom anxiously hastened forward to meet him.

"What's the matter, dad?" he asked as cheerfully as he could. "Have you been figuring over that gyroscope problem again, against my express orders?" and he laughed a little.

"No, Tom, it's not the gyroscope that's worrying me."

"What is it then?"

"Those scoundrels are around again, Tom!" and Mr. Swift looked apprehensively about him.

"You mean the men who stole the turbine model?"

"Yes. I was walking in the woods near the hotel yesterday and I saw Anson Morse. He did not see me, for I turned aside as quickly as I had a glimpse of him. He was talking to another man."

"What sort of a man?"

"Well, an ordinary enough individual, but I noticed that he had tattooed on the little finger of his left hand a blue ring."

"Happy Harry, the tramp!" exclaimed Tom. "What can he and Morse be doing here?"

"I don't know, Tom, but I'm worried. I wish I was back home. I'm afraid something may happen to some of my inventions. I want to go back to Shopton, Tom."

"Nonsense, dad. Don't worry just because you saw some of your former enemies. Everything is all right at home. Mrs. Baggert and Garret Jackson will look after things. But, if you like, I can find out for you how matters are."

"How, Tom?"

"By taking a run down there in my motor-boat. I can do it to-morrow and get back by night, if I start early. Then you will not worry."

"All right, Tom; I wish you would. Come up to my room and we will talk it over. I'd rather have you go than telephone, as I don't like to talk of my business over the wire if I can avoid it."

CHAPTER X

A CRY FOR HELP

"Now, dad, tell me all about it," requested Tom when he and Ned were in Mr. Swift's apartment at the hotel, safe from the rain that was falling. "How did you happen to see Anson Morse and Happy Harry?" My old readers will doubtless remember that the latter was the disguised tramp who was so vindictive toward Tom, while Morse was the man who endeavored to sneak in Mr. Swift's shop and steal a valuable invention.

"Well, Tom," proceeded the inventor, "there isn't much to tell. I was out walking in the woods yesterday, and when I was behind a clump of bushes I heard voices. I looked out and there I saw the two men.

"At first I thought they were trailing me, but I saw that they had not seen me, and I didn't see how they could know I was in the neighborhood. So I quietly made my way back to the hotel."

"Could you hear what they were saying?"

"Not all, but they seemed angry over something. The man with the blue ring on his finger asked the other man whether Murdock had been heard from."

"Who is Murdock?"

"I don't know, unless he is another member of the gang or unless that is an assumed name."

"It may be that. What else did you hear?"

"The man we know as Morse replied that he hadn't heard from him, but that he suspected Murdock was playing a double game. Then the tramp—Happy Harry—asked this question: 'Have you any clew to the sparkler?' And Morse answered: 'No, but I think Murdock has hid it somewhere and is trying to get away with it without giving us our share.' Then the two men walked away, and I came back to the hotel," finished Mr. Swift.

"Sparkler," murmured Tom. "I wonder what that can be?"

"That's a slang word for diamonds," suggested Ned.

"So it is. In that case, dad, I think we have nothing to worry about. Those fellows must be going to commit a diamond robbery or perhaps it has already taken place."

The inventor seemed relieved at this theory of his son. His face brightened and he said:

"If they are going to commit a robbery, Tom, we ought to notify the police."

"But if they said that 'Murdock,' whoever he is, had the sparkler and was trying to get away with it without giving them their share, wouldn't that indicate that the robbery had aleady taken place?" asked Ned.

"That's so," agreed Tom. "But it won't do any harm to tell the hotel detective that suspicious characters are around, no matter if the robbery has been committed. Then he can be on the lookout. But I don't think we have anything to worry about, dad. Still, if you like, I'll take a run down to the house to see that everything is all right, though I'm sure it will be found that we have nothing to be alarmed over."

"Well, I will be more relieved if you do," said the inventor. "However, suppose we have a good supper now and you boys can stay at the hotel to-night. Then you and Ned can start off early in the morning."

"All right," agreed Tom, but there was a thoughtful look on his face and he appeared to be planning something that needed careful attention to details.

After supper that night Tom took his chum to one side and asked:

"Would you mind very much if you didn't make the trip to Shopton with me?"

"No, Tom, of course not, if it will help you any. Do you want me to stay here?"

"I think it will be a good plan. I don't like to leave dad alone if those scoundrels are around. Of course he's able to look after himself, but sometimes he gets absent minded from thinking too much about his inventions."

"Of course I'll stay here at the hotel. This is just as good a vacation as I could wish."

"Oh, I don't mean all the while. Just a day or so—until I come back. I may be here again by to-morrow night and find that my father is needlessly alarmed. Then something may have happened at home and I would be delayed. If I should be, I'd feel better to know that you were here."

"Then I'll stay, and if I see any cf those men——"

"You'd better steer clear of them," advised Tom quickly. "They are dangerous customers."

"All right. Then I'll go over and give Miss Nestor lessons on how to run a motor-boat," was the smiling response. "I fancy, with what she and I know, we can make out pretty well."

"Hold on there!" cried Tom gaily. "No trespassing, you know."

"Oh, I'll just say I'm your agent," promised Ned with a grin. "You can't object to that."

"No, I s'pose not. Well, do the best you can. She is certainly a nice girl."

"Yes, but you do seem to turn up at most opportune times. Luck is certainly with you where she is concerned. First you save her in a runaway——"

"After I start the runaway," interrupted Tom.

"Then you take her for a ride in your motor-boat, and, lastly, you come to her relief when she is stalled in the middle of the lake. Oh, you certainly are a lucky dog!"

"Never mind, I'm giving you a show. Now let's get to bed early, as I want to get a good start."

Tom awoke to find a nasty, drizzling rainstorm in progress, and the lake was almost hidden from view by a swirling fog. Still he was not to be daunted from his trip to Shopton by the weather, and, after a substantial breakfast, he bade his father and Ned good-by and started off in the *Arrow*.

The canopy he had provided was an efficient protection against the rain, a celluloid window in the forward hanging curtains affording him a view so that he could steer.

Through the mist puffed the boat, the motor

being throttled down to medium speed, for Tom was not as familiar with the lake as he would like to have been, and he did not want to run aground or into another craft.

He was thinking over what his father had told him about the presence of the men and vainly wondering what might be their reference to the "sparkler." His thoughts also dwelt on the curious removal of the bracing block from under the gasoline tank of his boat.

"I shouldn't be surprised but what Andy Foger did that," he mused. "Some day he and I will have a grand fight, and then maybe he'll let me alone. Well, I've got other things to think about now. The hotel detective can keep a lookout for the men around the hotel, after the warning I gave him, and I'll see that all is right at home."

The fog lifted somewhat and Tom put on more speed. As he was steering the boat along near shore he heard, off to the woods at his right, the report of a gun. It came so suddenly that he jumped involuntarily. A moment later there sounded, plainly through the damp air, a cry for help.

"Some one's hurt—shot!" cried the youth aloud.

He turned the boat in toward the bank. As he

shut off the power from the motor he heard the cry again:

"Help! help! help!"

"I must go ashore!" he exclaimed. "Probably some one is badly wounded by a gun."

He paused for a moment as the fear came to him that it might be some of the patent thieves. Then, dismissing that idea as the *Arrow's* prow touched the gravel, Tom sprang out, drew the boat up a little way, fastened the rope to a tree and hurried off into the dripping woods in the direction of the voice that was calling for aid.

CHAPTER XI

A QUICK RUN

"WHERE are you?" cried Tom. "Are you hurt? Where are you?"

Uttering these words after he had hurried into the woods a short distance, the young inventor paused for an answer. At first he could hear nothing but the drip of water from the branches of the trees; then, as he listened intently, he became aware of a groan not far away.

"Where are you?" cried the lad again. "I've come to help you. Where are you?"

He had lost what little fear he had had at first, that it might be one of the unscrupulous gang, and came to the conclusion that he might safely offer to help.

Once more the groan sounded and it was followed by a faint voice speaking:

"Here I am, under the big oak tree. Oh, whoever you are, help me quickly! I'm bleeding to death!"

With the sound of the voice to guide him, Tom swung around. The appeal had come from the left and, looking in that direction, he saw, through the mist, a large oak tree. Leaping over the underbrush toward it he caught sight of the wounded man at its foot. Beside him lay a gun and there was a wound in the man's right arm.

"Who shot you?" cried Tom, hurrying to the side of the man. "Was it some of those patent thieves?" Then, realizing that a stranger would know nothing of the men who had stolen the model, Tom prepared to change the form of his question. But, before he had an opportunity to do this, the man, whose eyes were closed, opened them, and, as he got a better sight of his face, Tom uttered a cry.

"Why, it's Mr. Duncan!" exclaimed the lad. He had recognized the rich hunter, whom he had first met in the woods that spring shortly after Happy Harry, the tramp, had disabled Tom's motor-cycle. "Mr. Duncan," the young inventor repeated, "how did you get shot?"

"Is that you, Tom Swift?" asked the gunner. "Help me, please. I must stop this bleeding in my arm. I'll tell you about it afterward. Wind something around it tight—your handkerchief will do."

The man sighed weakly and his eyes closed

again. The lad saw the blood spurting from an ugly wound.

"I must make a tourniquet," the youth exclaimed. "That will check the bleeding until I can get him to a doctor."

With Tom to think was to act. He took out his knife and cut off Mr. Duncan's sleeves below the injury, slashing through coat and shirts. Then he saw that part of a charge of shot had torn away some of the large muscular development of the upper arm. The hunter seemed to have fainted and the youth worked quickly. Tying his handkerchief above the wound and inserting a small stone under the cloth, so that the pebble would press on the main artery, Tom put a stick in the handkerchief and began to twist it. This had the effect of tightening the linen around the arm, and in a few seconds the lad was glad to see that the blood had stopped spurting out with every beat of the heart. Giving the tourniquet a few more twists to completely stop the flow of blood, Tom fastened the stick-lever in place by a bit of string.

"That's—that's better," murmured Mr. Duncan. "Now if you can go for a doctor——" he had to pause for breath.

"I'll not leave you here alone while I go for a doctor," declared Tom. "I have my motor-boat

on the lake. Do you think I could get you down
to it and take you home?"

"Perhaps—maybe. I'll be stronger in a moment, now that the bleeding has stopped. But
not—not home—frighten my wife. Take me to
the sanitarium if you can—sanitarium up the lake,
a few miles from here."

The unfortunate man, who had tried to sit upright, had to lean back against the tree again.
Tom understood what he meant in spite of the
broken sentences. Mr. Duncan did not want to
be taken home in the condition he was then in, for
fear of alarming his wife. He wanted to be taken
to the sanitarium, and Tom knew where this was,
a well-known resort for the treatment of various
diseases and surgical cases. It was about five
miles away and on the opposite shore of the lake.

"Water—a drink!" murmured Mr. Duncan.

Seeing that his patient would be all right, for a
few minutes at least, Tom hurried to his motor-
boat, got a cup and, filling it with water from a
jug he carried, he hastened with it to the hunter.
The fluid revived the man wonderfully and now
that the bleeding had almost completely stopped,
Mr. Duncan was much stronger.

"Do you think you can get to the boat, if I help
you?" asked Tom.

"Yes, I believe so. To think of meeting you

again, and under such circumstances! It is providential."

"Did some one shoot you?" inquired Tom, who could not get out of his head the notion of the men who had once assaulted him.

"No, I shot myself," answered Mr. Duncan as he got to his feet with Tom's help. "I was out with my gun, practicing just as I was that day when I met you in the woods. I stooped down to crawl under a bush and the weapon went off, the muzzle being close against my arm. I can't understand how it happened. I fell down and called for help. Then I guess I must have fainted, but I came to when I heard you talking to me. I shouldn't have come out to-day as it is so wet, but I had some new shot shells I wished to try in order to test them before the hunting season. But if I can get to the sanitarium, I will be well taken care of. I know one of the doctors there."

With Tom leading him and acting as a sort of support, the journey to the motor-boat was slowly made. Making as comfortable a bed as possible out of the seat cushions, Tom assisted Mr. Duncan to it, and then starting the engine he sent his boat out from shore at half speed, as the fog was still thick and he did not want to run upon a rock.

"Do you know where the sanitarium is?" asked the wounded hunter.

"About," answered Tom a little doubtfully, "but I'm afraid it's going to be hard to locate it in this fog."

"There's a compass in my coat pocket," said Mr. Duncan. "Take it out and I'll tell you how to steer. You ought to carry a compass if you're going to be a sailor."

Tom was beginning to think so himself and wondered that he had not thought of it before. He found the one the hunter had, and placing it on the seat near him, he carefully listened to the wounded man's directions. Tom easily comprehended and soon had the boat headed in the proper direction. After that it was comparatively easy to keep on the right course, even in the fog.

But there was another danger, however, and this was that he might run into another boat. True, there were not many on Lake Carlopa, but there were some, and one of the few motor-boats might be out in spite of the bad weather.

"Guess I'll not run at full speed," decided Tom. "I wouldn't like to crash into the *Red Streak*. We'd both sink."

So he did not run his motor at the limit and sat at the steering-wheel, peering ahead into the fog for the first sight of another craft.

He turned to look at Mr. Duncan and was alarmed at the pallor of his face. The man's eyes were closed and he was breathing in a peculiar manner.

"Mr. Duncan," cried Tom, "are you worse?"

There was no answer. Leaving the helm for a moment, Tom bent over the injured hunter. A glance showed him what had happened. The tourniquet had slipped and the wound was bleeding again. Tom quickly shut off the motor, so that he might give his whole attention to the work of tightening the handkerchief. But something seemed to be wrong. No matter how tightly he twisted the stick the blood did not stop flowing. The lad was frightened. In a short time the man would bleed to death.

"I've got to get him to the sanitarium in record time!" exclaimed Tom. "Fog or no fog, I've got to run at full speed! I've got to chance it!"

Making the bandage as tight as he could and fastening it in place, the young inventor sprang to the motor and set it in motion. Then he went to the wheel. In a few minutes the *Arrow* was speeding through the water as it had never done before, except when it had raced the *Red Streak*. "If I hit anything—good-by!" thought Tom grimly. His hands were tense on the rim of the steering-wheel and he was ready in an instant to reverse the motor as he sat there straining his eyes to see through the curtain of mist that hung over the lake. Now and then he glanced at the compass, to keep on the right course, and from time to time he looked at Mr. Duncan. The hunter was still unconscious.

How Tom accomplished that trip he hardly remembered afterward. Through the fog he shot, expecting any moment to crash into some other boat. He did pass a rowing craft in which sat a lone fisherman. The lad was upon him in an instant, but a turn of the wheel sent the *Arrow* safely past, and the startled fisherman, whose frail craft was set to rocking violently by the swell from the motor-boat, sent an objecting cry through the fog after Tom. But the youth did not reply. On and on he raced, getting the last atom of power from his motor.

He feared Mr. Duncan would be dead when he arrived, but when he saw the dock of the sanitarium looming up out of the mist and shut off the power to slowly run up to it, he placed his hand on the wounded man's heart and found it still beating.

"He's alive, anyhow," thought the youth, and then his craft bumped up against the bulkhead and a man in the boathouse on the dock was sent on the run for a physician.

Mr. Duncan was quickly taken up to the sanitarium on a stretcher and Tom followed.

"You must have made a record run," observed one of the physicians a little while afterward, when Tom was telling of his trip while waiting in the office to hear the report on the hunter's condition.

"I guess I did," muttered the young inventor "only I didn't think so at the time. It seemed as if we were only crawling along."

CHAPTER XII

SUSPICIOUS CHARACTERS

UNDER the skill of the physicians at the lake sanitarium Mr. Duncan's wound was quickly attended to and the bleeding, which Tom had partly checked, was completely stopped. Some medicines having been administered, the hunter regained a little of his strength, and, about an hour after he had been brought to the resort, he was able to see Tom, who, at his request, was admitted to his room. The young inventor found Mr. Duncan propped up in bed, with his injured arm bandaged.

"Is the injury a bad one?" asked Tom, entering softly.

"Not as bad as I feared," replied the hunter, while a trained nurse placed a chair for the lad at the bedside. "If it had not been for you, though, I'm afraid to think of what might have happened."

"I am glad I chanced to be going past when you called," replied the lad.

"Well, you can imagine how thankful *I* am," resumed Mr. Duncan. "I'll thank you more properly at another time. I hope I didn't delay you on your trip."

"It's not of much consequence," responded the youth. "I was only going to see that everything was all right at our house," and he explained about his father being at the hotel and mentioned his worriment. "I will go on now unless I can do something more for you," resumed Tom. "I will probably stay at our house all night to-night instead of trying to get back to Sandport."

"I'd like to send word to my wife about what has happened," said the hunter. "If it would not be too much out of your way, I'd appreciate it if you could stop at my home in Waterford and tell her, so she will not be alarmed at my absence."

"I'll do it," replied our hero. "There is no special need of my hurrying. I have brought your gun and compass up from the boat. They are down in the office."

"Will you do me a favor?" asked Mr. Duncan quickly.

"Of course."

"Then please accept that gun and compass with my compliments. They are both of excellent make, and I don't think I shall use that gun this season. My wife would be superstitious about it. As for the compass, you'll need one in this fog, and I can recommend mine as being accurate."

"Oh, I couldn't think of taking them," expostulated Tom, but his eyes sparkled in anticipation, for he had been wishing for a gun such as Mr. Duncan owned. He also needed a compass.

"If you don't take them I shall feel very much offended," the hunter said, "and the nurse here will tell you that sick persons ought to be humored. Hadn't they?" and he appealed to the pretty young woman, who was smiling at Tom.

"That's perfectly true," she said, showing her white, even teeth. "I think, Mr. Swift, I shall have to order you to take them."

"All right," agreed Tom, "only it's too much for what I did."

"It isn't half enough," remarked Mr. Duncan solemnly. "Just explain matters to my wife, if you will, and tell her the doctor says I can be out in about a week. But I'm not going hunting or practicing shots again."

A little later Tom, with the compass before him to guide him on his course through the fog, was speeding his boat toward Waterford. Now and then he glanced at the fine shotgun which he had so unexpectedly acquired.

"This will come in dandy this fall!" he exclaimed. "I'll go hunting quail and partridge as well as wild ducks. This compass is just what I need, too."

Mrs. Duncan was at first very much alarmed when Tom started to tell her of the accident, but she soon calmed down as the lad went more into details and stated how comparatively out of danger her husband now was. The hunter's wife insisted that Tom remain to dinner, and as he had made up his mind he would have to devote two days instead of one to the trip to his house, he consented.

The fog lifted that afternoon, and Tom, rejoicing in the sunlight, which drove away the storm clouds, speeded up the *Arrow* until she was skimming over the lake like a shaft from a bow.

"This is something like," he exclaimed. "I'll soon be at home, find everything all right and telephone to dad. Then I'll sleep in my own room and start back in the morning."

When Tom was within a few miles of his own boathouse he heard behind him the "put-put" of a motor craft. Turning, he saw the *Red Streak* fairly flying along at some distance from him.

"Andy certainly is getting the speed out of her now," he remarked. "He'd beat me if we were racing, but the trouble with his boat and engine is that he can't always depend on it. I guess he doesn't understand how to run it. I wonder if he'll offer to race now?"

But the red-haired owner of the auto boat evidently did not intend to offer Tom a race. The *Red Streak* went on down the lake, passing the *Arrow* about half a mile away. Then the young inventor saw that Andy had two other lads in the boat with him.

"Sam Snedecker and Pete Bailey, I guess," he murmured. "Well, they're a trio pretty much alike. The farther off they are the better I like it."

Tom once more gave his attention to his own boat. He was going at a fair speed, but not the limit, and he counted on reaching home in about a half hour. Suddenly, when he was just congratulating himself on the smooth-running qualities of his motor, which had not missed an explosion, the machinery stopped.

"Hello!" exclaimed the young inventor in some alarm. "What's up now?"

He quickly shut off the gasoline and went back to the motor. Now there are so many things that may happen to a gasoline engine that it would be difficult to name them all offhand, and Tom, who had not had very much experience, was at a loss to find what had stopped his machinery. He tried the spark and found that by touching the wire to the top of the cylinder, when the proper connection was made, that he had a hot, "fat one." The compression seemed all right and the supply pipe from the gasoline tank was in perfect order. Still the motor would not go. No explosion resulted when he turned the fly-wheel over, not even when he primed the cylinder by putting a little gasoline in through the cocks on the cylinder heads.

"That's funny," he remarked to himself as he rested from his labors and contemplated the "dead" motor. "First time it has gone back on me." The boat was drifting down the lake, and, at the sound of another motor craft approaching, Tom looked up. He saw the *Red Streak*, containing Andy Foger and his cronies. They had observed the young inventor's plight.

"Want a tow?" sneered Andy.

"What'll you take for your second-hand boat that won't run?" asked Pete Bailey.

"Better get out of the way or you might be run down," added Sam Snedecker.

Tom was too angry and chagrined to reply, and the *Red Streak* swept on.

"I'll make her go, if it takes all night!" declared Tom energetically. Once more he tried to start the motor. It coughed and sighed, as if in protest, but would not explode. Then Tom cried: "The spark plug! That's where the trouble is, I'll wager. Why didn't I think of it before?"

It was the work of but a minute to unscrew the spark plugs from the tops of the cylinders. He found that both had such accumulations of carbon on them that no spark could ever have reached the mixture of gasoline and air.

"I'll put new ones in," he decided, for he carried a few spare plugs for emergencies. Inside of five minutes, with the new plugs in place, the motor was running better than before.

"Now for home!" cried Tom, "and if I meet Andy Foger I'll race him this time."

But the *Red Streak* was not in sight, and, a little later, Tom had run the *Arrow* into the boat-house, locked the door and was on his way up to the mansion.

"I suppose Mrs. Baggert and Garret will be surprised to see me," he remarked. "Maybe they'll think we don't trust them, by coming back in this fashion to see that everything is safe. But then, I suppose, dad is naturally nervous about some of his valuable machinery and inventions. I think I'll find everything all right, though."

As Tom went up the main path and swung off to a side one, which was a short cut to the house, he saw in the dusk, for it was now early evening, a movement in the bushes that lined the walk.

"Hello, Garret!" exclaimed the lad, taking it

for granted it was the engineer employed by Mr. Swift.

There was no reply, and Tom, with a sudden suspicion, sprang toward the bushes. The shrubbery was more violently agitated and, as the lad reached the screen of foliage, he saw a man spring up from the ground and take to his heels.

"Here! Who are you? What do you want?" yelled Tom.

Hardly had he spoken when from behind a big apple tree another man sprung. It was light enough so that the lad could see his face, and a glimpse of it caused him to cry out:

"Happy Harry, the tramp!"

Before he could call again the two men had disappeared.

CHAPTER XIII

TOM IN DANGER

"GARRET! Garret Jackson!" cried Tom as he struggled through the hedge of bushes and ran after the men. "Where are you, Garret? Come on and help me chase these men!"

But there came no answer to Tom's hail. He could not hear the sound of the retreating footsteps of the men now and concluded that they had made their escape. Still he would not give up, but dashed on, slipping and stumbling, now and then colliding with a tree.

"What can they be doing here?" thought Tom in great anxiety. "Are they after some more of dad's inventions because they didn't get his turbine motor?"

"Hello! Who's there? Who are you?" called a voice suddenly.

"Oh, Garret! Where have you been?" asked the young inventor, recognizing the tones of his father's keeper. "I've been calling you. Some of those scoundrels are around again!"

"Why if it isn't Tom!" ejaculated the engineer. "However in the world did you get here? I thought you were at Sandport."

"I'll explain later, Garret. Just now I want to catch those men, if I can."

"Which men?"

"Happy Harry and another one. I saw them hiding down by the orchard path. Come on, they're right ahead of us."

But though they hunted as well as they were able to in the fast-gathering darkness, there was no trace of the intruders. They had to give up, and Tom, after going to the boathouse to see that the *Arrow* was all right, returned to the house, where he told the engineer and housekeeper what had brought him back and how he had surprised the two men.

"Is everything all right, Garret?" he concluded. "Dad is nervous and frightened. I must telephone him at the hotel to-night and let him know, for I promised to come back. I can't, though, until to-morrow."

"Everything is all right as far as I know," answered Jackson. "I've kept a careful watch and the burglar alarm has been in working order. Mrs. Baggert and I haven't been disturbed a single night since you went away. It's curious

that the men should be here the very night you
come back. Maybe they followed you."

"I hardly think so, for they didn't know I was
coming."

"You can't tell what those fellows know," commented the engineer. "But, anyhow, I don't
s'pose they could have gotten here from Sandport
as soon as you did."

"Oh, yes they could, in their automobile," declared Tom. "But I don't believe they knew I was
coming. They knew we were away, however,
and thought it would be a good time to steal
something, I guess. Are you sure nothing has
been taken?"

"Perfectly sure, but you and I will take a look
around the shop."

They made a hasty examination, but found
nothing disturbed and no signs that any one had
tried to break in.

"I think I'll telephone dad that everything is
all right," decided Tom. "It is, as far as his inventions are concerned, and if I tell about seeing
the men it will only worry him. I can explain
that part better when I see him. But when I go
back, Garret, you will have to be on your guard,
since those men are in the neighborhood."

"I will, Tom. Don't worry."

Mr. Swift was soon informed by his son over

the telephone that nothing in the shops had been disturbed, and the inventor received the news with evident satisfaction. He requested Tom to come back to the hotel in the morning, in order that the three of them might go for a ride about the lake in the afternoon, and Tom decided to make an early start.

The night passed without incident, though Tom, who kept the gun Mr. Duncan had given him in readiness for use, got up several times, thinking he heard suspicious noises. After an early breakfast, and having once more cautioned the engineer and housekeeper to be on their guard, Tom started back in the *Arrow*.

As it would not be much out of his way, the young inventor decided to cut across the lake and stop at the sanitarium, that he might inquire about Mr. Duncan. He thought he could speed the *Arrow* up sufficiently to make up for any time he might lose, and, with this in mind, he headed out toward the middle of Lake Carlopa. The engine was working splendidly with the new spark plugs, and Tom was wondering if there was any possible method of getting more revolutions out of the motor. He had about come to the conclusion that a new propeller might answer his purpose when he heard the noise of an approaching boat. He looked up quickly and exclaimed:

"Andy Foger again, and Pete and Sam are with him. It's a wonder he wouldn't go off on a trip instead of cruising around so near home. Guess he's afraid he'll get stuck."

Idly Tom watched the *Red Streak*. It was cutting through the water at a fast rate, throwing up curling foam on either side of the sharp bow.

"He seems to be heading this way," mused Tom. "Well, I'm not going to race with him to-day."

Nearer and nearer came the speedy craft, straight for the *Arrow*. The young inventor shifted his helm in order to get out of Andy's course, but to his surprise he saw that the red-haired lad changed the direction of his own boat.

"Guess he wants to see how close he can come to me," thought our hero. "Maybe he wants to show how fast he's going."

The *Red Streak* was now so close that the features of the occupants could easily be distinguished. There were grins on the faces of Andy and his cronies.

"Get out of the way or we'll run you down!" cried the bully. "We've got the right of way."

"Don't you try anything like that!" shouted Tom in some alarm, not that he was afraid of Andy, but the *Red Streak* was getting dangerously near, and he knew Andy was not a skilful helmsman. The auto-boat was now headed directly at the *Arrow* and coming on speedily. Andy was bending over the wheel and Tom had begun to turn his, in order to get well out of the way of the insolent, squint-eyed lad and his friends.

Suddenly Andy uttered a cry and leaped up.

"Look out! look out!" he yelled. "My steering gear has broken! I can't change my course. Look out!"

The *Red Streak* was bearing right down on Tom's boat.

"Shut off your power! Reverse!" shouted Tom.

Andy seemed confused and did not know what to do. Sam Snedecker sprang to the side of his crony, but he knew even less about a motor-boat. It looked as if Tom would be run down, and he was in great danger.

But the young inventor did not lose his head. He put his wheel hard over and then, leaping to his motor, sent it full speed forward. Not a moment too soon had he acted, for an instant later the other boat shot past the stern of the *Arrow,* hitting it a severe but glancing blow. Tom's boat quivered from end to end and he quickly shut off the power. By this time Andy had succeeded in slowing down his craft. The young inventor hastily looked over the side of the *Arrow*. One of the rudder fastenings had been torn loose.

"What do you mean by running me down?" shouted Tom angrily.

"I—I didn't do it on purpose," returned Andy contritely. "I was seeing how near I could come to you when my steering gear broke. I hope I haven't damaged you."

"My rudder's broken," went on Tom, "and I've got to put back to repair it. I ought to have you arrested for this!"

"I'll pay for the damage," replied Andy, and he was so frightened that he was white, in spite of his tan and freckles.

"That won't do me any good now," retorted Tom. "It will delay me a couple of hours. If you try any tricks like that again, I'll complain to the authorities and you won't be allowed to run a boat on this lake."

Andy knew that his rival was in the right and did not reply. The bully and his cronies busied themselves over the broken steering gear, and the young inventor, finding that he could make a shift to get back to his boathouse, turned his craft around and headed for there, in order to repair the damage.

CHAPTER XIV

THE ARROW DISAPPEARS

PAYING no heed to the occupants of the bully's boat, who, by reason of their daring, had been responsible for his accident that might have resulted seriously, Tom was soon at his dock. He had it conveniently arranged for hoisting craft out of the water to repair them, and in a few minutes the stern of the *Arrow* was elevated so that he could get at the rudder.

"Well, it's not as bad as I thought," he remarked when, with critical eye, he had noted the damage done. I can fix it in about an hour if Garret helps me."

Going up to the house to get some tools and to tell the engineer that he had returned, Tom looked out over the lake and saw Andy's boat moving slowly off.

"They've got her fixed up in some kind of shape," he murmured. "It's a shame for a chump like Andy to have a good boat like that. He'll spoil it in one season. He's getting altogether too reckless. First thing he knows, he and I will have a clash and I'll pay back some of the old scores."

Mr. Jackson was much surprised to see the young inventor home again so soon, as was also Mrs. Baggert. Tom explained what had happened, and he and the engineer went to work repairing the damage done by the *Red Streak*. As the owner of the *Arrow* had anticipated, the work did not take long, and, shortly before dinner time, the boat was ready to resume the interrupted trip to Sandport.

"Better stay and have lunch," urged Mrs. Baggert. "You can hardly get to the hotel by night, anyhow, and maybe it would be better not to start until to-morrow."

"No, I must get back to-night or dad would be worried," declared Tom. "I've been gone longer now than I calculated on. But I will have dinner here, and, if necessary, I can do the last half of the trip after dark. I know the way now and I have a compass and a good searchlight."

The *Arrow* was let down into the water again and tied outside the boathouse ready for a quick start. The dinner Mrs. Baggert provided was so good that Tom lingered over it longer than he meant to, and he asked for a second apple dumpling with hard sauce on. So it was with a very comfortable feeling indeed and with an almost forgiving spirit toward Andy Foger that our hero started down the path to the lake.

"Now for a quick run to Sandport," he said aloud. "I hope I shan't see any more of those men and that dad hasn't been bothered by them. His suspicions about the house weren't altogether unfounded, for I did see the tramp and some one else sneaking around, but I don't believe they'll come back now."

Tom swung around the path that led to the dock. As he came in sight of the water, he stared as if he could not believe what he saw, or, rather, what he did not see. For there was no craft tied to the string-piece, where he had fastened his motor-boat. He looked again, rubbed his eyes to make sure and then cried out:

"The *Arrow* is gone!"

There was no doubt of it. The craft was not at the dock. Breaking into a run, Tom hastened to the boathouse. The *Arrow* was not in there, and a look across the lake showed only a few rowboats in sight.

"That's mighty funny," mused the youth. "I wonder——"

He paused suddenly in his thoughts.

"Maybe Garret took it out to try and see that it worked all right," he said hopefully. "He knows how to run a boat. Maybe he wanted to see how the rudder behaved and is out in it now. He got through dinner before I did. But I should have thought he'd have said something to me if he was going out in it."

This was the one weak point in Tom's theory, and he felt it at once.

"I'll see if Garret is in his shop," he went on as he turned back toward the house.

The first person he met as he headed for the group of small structures where Mr. Swift's inventive work was carried on was Garret Jackson, the engineer.

"I—I thought you were out in my boat!" stammered Tom.

"Your boat! Why would I be out in your boat?" and Mr. Jackson removed his pipe from his mouth and stared at the young inventor.

"Because it's gone!"

"Gone!" repeated the engineer, and then Tom told him. The two hurried down to the dock, but the addition of another pair of eyes was of no assistance in locating the *Arrow*. The trim little motor craft was nowhere to be seen.

"I can't understand it," said Tom helplessly. "I wasn't gone more than an hour at dinner, and yet——"

"It doesn't take long to steal a motor-boat," commented the engineer.

"But I think I would have heard them start it," went on the lad. "Maybe it drifted off, though I'm sure I tied it securely."

"No, there's not much likelihood of that. There's no wind to-day and no currents in the lake. But it could easily have been towed off by some one in a rowboat and then you would not have heard the motor start."

"That's so," agreed the youth. "That's probably how they did it. They sneaked up here in a rowboat and towed the *Arrow* off. I'm sure of it."

"And I'll wager I know who did it," exclaimed Mr. Jackson energetically.

"Who?" demanded Tom quickly.

"Those men who were sneaking around— Happy Harry and his gang. They stole the boat once and they'd do it again. Those men took your boat, Tom."

The young inventor shook his head.

"No," he answered, "I don't believe they did."

"Why not?"

"Well, because they wouldn't dare come back here when they knew we're on the lookout for them. It would be too risky."

"Oh, those fellows don't care for risk," was the

opinion of Mr. Jackson. "Take my word for it, they have your boat. They have been keeping watch, and as soon as they saw the dock unprotected they sneaked up and stole the *Arrow.*"

"I don't think so," repeated Mr. Swift's son.

"Who do you think took it, then?"

"Andy Foger!" was the quick response. "I believe he and his cronies did it to annoy me. They have been trying to get even with me—or at least Andy has—for outbidding him on this boat. He's tried several times, but he hasn't succeeded—until now. I'm sure Andy Foger has my boat," and Tom, with a grim tightening of his lips, swung around as though to start in instant pursuit.

"Where are you going?" asked Mr. Jackson.

"To find Andy and his cronies. When I locate them I'll make them tell me where my boat is."

"Hadn't you better send some word to your father? You can hardly get to Sandport now, and he'll be worried about you."

"That's so, I will. I'll telephone dad that the boat—no, I'll not do that either, for he'd only worry and maybe get sick. I'll just tell him I've had a little accident, that Andy ran into me and that I can't come back to the hotel for a day or two. Maybe I'll be lucky to find my boat in that time. But dad won't worry then, and, when I see him, I can explain. ' That's what I'll do," and Tom was soon talking to Mr. Swift by telephone.

The inventor was very sorry his son could not come back to rejoin him and Ned, but there was no help for it, and, with as cheerful voice as he could assume, the lad promised to start for Sandport at the earliest opportunity.

"Now to find Andy and my boat!" Tom exclaimed as he hung up the telephone receiver.

CHAPTER XV

A DISMAYING STATEMENT

TROUBLE is sometimes good in a way; it makes a person resourceful. Tom Swift had had his share of annoyances of late, but they had served a purpose. He had learned to think clearly and quickly. Now, when he found his boat stolen, he at once began to map out a plan of action.

"What will you do first?" asked Mr. Jackson as he saw his employer's son hesitating.

"First I'm going to Andy Foger's house," declared the young inventor. "If he's home I'm going to tell him what I think of him. If he's not, I'm going to find him."

"Why don't you take your sailboat and run down to his dock?" suggested the engineer. "It isn't as quick as your motor-boat, but it's better than walking."

"So it is," exclaimed the lad. "I *will* use my catboat. I had forgotten all about it of late. I'm glad you spoke."

He was soon sailing down the lake in the direction of the boathouse on the water front of Mr. Foger's property. It needed but a glance around the dock to show him that the *Red Streak* was not there, but Tom recollected the accident to the steering gear and thought perhaps Andy had taken his boat to some wharf where there was a repair shop and there left it to return home himself. But inquiry of Mrs. Foger, who was as nice a woman as her son was a mean lad, gave Tom the information that his enemy was not at home.

"He telephoned to me that his boat was damaged," said Mrs. Foger gently, "and that he had taken it to get fixed. Then, he said, he and some friends were going on a little cruise and might not be back to-night."

"Did he say where he was going?" asked our hero, who did not tell Andy's mother why he wanted to see her son.

"No, and I'm worried about him. Sometimes I think Andy is too—well, too impetuous, and I'm afraid he will get into trouble."

Tom, in spite of his trouble, could hardly forbear smiling. Andy's mother was totally unaware of the mean traits of her son and thought him a very fine chap. Tom was not going to undeceive her.

"I'm afraid something will happen to him," she

went on. "Do you think there is any danger being out on the lake in a motor-boat, Mr. Swift? I understand you have one."

"Yes, I have one," answered Tom. He was going to say he had once had one, but thought better of it. "No, there is very little danger this time of year," he added.

"I am very glad to hear you say so," went on Mrs. Foger with a sigh. "I shall feel more at ease when Andy is away now. When he returns home, I shall tell him you called upon him and he will return your visit. I am glad to see that the custom of paying calls has not died out among the present generation. It is a pleasant habit, and I am glad to have my son conform to it. He shall return your kind visit."

"Oh, no, it's of no consequence," replied Tom quickly, thinking grimly that his visit was far from a friendly one. "There is no need to tell your son I was here. I will probably see him in a day or two."

"Oh, but I shall tell him." insisted Mrs. Foger with a kind smile. "I'm sure he will appreciate your call."

There was much doubt concerning this in the mind of the young inventor, but he did not express it and soon took his leave. Up and down the lake for the rest of the day he cruised, looking in vain for a sight of Andy Foger in the *Red Streak*, but the racing boat appeared to be well hidden.

"If I only could find where they've taken mine," mused Tom. "Hang it all, this is rotten luck!" and for the first time he began to feel discouraged.

"Maybe you'd better notify the police," suggested Mr. Jackson when Tom returned to the Swift house that night. "They might help you locate it."

"I think I can do as well as the police," answered the youth. "If the boat is anywhere it's on the lake, and the police have no craft in which to make a search."

"That's so," agreed the engineer. "I wish I could help you, but I don't believe it would be wise for me to leave the house, especially since those men have been about lately."

"No, you must stay here," was Tom's opinion. "I'll take another day or two to search. By this time Andy and his gang will return, I'm sure, and I can tackle them."

"Suppose they don't?"

"Well, then I'll make a tour of the lake in my sailboat and I'll run up to Sandport and tell dad, for he will wonder what's keeping me. I'll know better next time than to leave my boat at the dock without taking out the connection at the spark coil, so no one can start the motor. I should have done that at first, but you always think of those things afterward."

The lad began his search again the next morning and cruised about in little bays and gulfs looking for a sight of the *Red Streak* or the *Arrow,* but he saw neither, and a call at Andy's house showed that the red-haired youth had not returned. Mrs. Foger was quite nervous over her son's continued absence, but Mr. Foger thought it was all right.

Another day passed without any results and the young inventor was getting so nervous, partly with worrying over the loss of his boat and partly on his father's account, that he did not know what to do.

"I can't stand it any longer," he announced to Mrs. Baggert the night of the third day, after a telephone message had been received from Mr. Swift. The inventor wanted to know why his son did not return to the hotel to join him and Ned.

"Well, what will you do?" asked the housekeeper.

"If I don't find my boat to-morrow, I'll sail to Sandport, bring home dad and Ned, and we three will go all over the lake. My boat must be on it somewhere, but Lake Carlopa is so cut up that it could easily be hidden."

"It's queer that the Foger boy doesn't come home. That makes it look as if he was guilty."

"Oh, I'm sure he took it all right," returned Tom. "All I want is to see him. It certainly is queer that he stays away as long as he does. Sam Snedecker and Pete Bailey are with him, too. But they'll have to return some time."

Tom dreamed that night of finding his boat and that it was a wreck. He awoke, glad to find that the latter part was not true, but wishing that some of his night vision might come to pass during the day.

He started out right after breakfast, and, as usual, headed for the Foger home. He almost disliked to ask Mrs. Foger if her son had yet returned, for Andy's mother was so polite and so anxious to know whether any danger threatened that Tom hardly knew how to answer her. But he was saved that embarrassment on this occasion, for as he was going up the walk from the lake to the residence he met the gardener and from him learned that Andy had not yet come back.

"But his mother had a message from him, I did hear," went on the man. "He's on his way. It seems he had some trouble."

"Trouble. What kind of trouble?" asked Tom.

"I don't rightly know, sir, but," and here the

gardener winked his eye, "Master Andy isn't particular what kind of trouble he gets into."

"That's right," agreed our hero, and as he went down again to where he had left his boat he thought: "Nor what kind of trouble he gets other people into. I wish I had hold of him for about five minutes!"

The sailboat swung slowly from the dock and heeled over to the gentle breeze. Hardly knowing what to do, Tom headed for the middle of the lake. He was discouraged and tired of making plans only to have them fail.

As he looked across the stretch of water he saw a boat coming toward him. He shaded his eyes with his hand to see better, and then, with a pair of marine glasses, took an observation. He uttered an exclamation.

"That's the *Red Streak* as sure as I'm alive!" he cried. "But what's the matter with her? They're rowing!"

The lad headed his boat toward the approaching one. There was no doubt about it. It was Andy Foger's craft, but it was not speeding forward under the power of the motor. Slowly and laboriously the occupants were pulling it along, and as it was not meant to be rowed, progress was very slow.

"They've had a breakdown," thought Tom.

"Serves 'em right! Now wait till I tackle 'em and find out where my boat is. I've a good notion to have Andy Foger arrested!"

The sailing craft swiftly approached the motor-boat. Tom could see the three occupants looking at him, apprehensively as well as curiously, he thought.

"Guess they didn't think I'd keep after 'em," mused the young inventor, and a little later he was beside the *Red Streak*.

"Well," cried Tom angrily, "it's about time you came back!"

"We've had a breakdown," remarked Andy, and he seemed quite humiliated. He was beginning to find out that he didn't know as much about a motor-boat as he thought he did.

"I've been waiting for you," went on Tom.

"Waiting for us? What for?" asked Sam Snedecker.

"What for? As if you didn't know!" blurted out the owner of the *Arrow*. "I want my boat, Andy Foger, the one you stole from me and hid! Tell me where it is at once or I'll have you arrested!"

"Your boat!" repeated the bully, and there was no mistaking the surprise in his tones.

"Yes, my boat! Don't try to bluff me like that."

"I'm not trying to bluff you. We've been away three days and just got back."

"Yes, I know you have. You took my boat with you, too."

"Are you crazy?" demanded Pete Bailey.

"No, but you fellows must have been to think you could take my boat and me not know it," and Tom, filled with wrath, grasped the gunwale of the *Red Streak* as if he feared it would suddenly shoot away.

"Look here!" burst out Andy, and he spoke sincerely, "we didn't touch your boat. Did we, fellows?"

"No!" exclaimed Sam and Pete at once, and they were very much in earnest.

"We didn't even know it was stolen, did we?" went on Andy.

"No," agreed his chums. Tom looked unconvinced.

"We haven't taken your boat and we can prove it," continued the bully. "I know you and I have had quarrels, but I'm telling you the truth, Tom Swift. I never touched your boat."

There was no mistaking the sincerity of Andy. He was not a skilful deceiver, and Tom, looking into his squint-eyes, which were opened unusually wide, could not but help believing the fellow.

"We haven't seen it since the day we had the

collision," added Andy, and his chums confirmed this statement.

"We went off on a little cruise," continued the red-haired bully, "and broke down several times. We had bad luck. Just as we were nearing home something went wrong with the engine again. I never saw such a poor motor. But we never took your boat, Tom Swift, and we can prove it."

Tom was in despair. He had been so sure that Andy was the thief, that to believe otherwise was difficult. Yet he felt that he must. He looked at the disabled motor of the *Red Streak* and viewed it with the interested and expert eye of a machinist, no matter if the owner of it was his enemy. Then suddenly a brilliant idea came into Tom's head.

CHAPTER XVI

STILL ON THE SEARCH

"You seem to have lots of trouble with your boat, Andy," said Tom after a few moments of rather embarrassed silence.

"I do," admitted the owner of the *Red Streak*. "I've had bad luck ever since I got it, but usually I've been able to fix it by looking in the book. This time I can't find out what the trouble is, nor can any of the fellows. It stopped when we were out in the middle of the lake and we had to row. I'm sick of motor-boating."

"Suppose I fix it for you?" went on Tom.

"If you do, I'll pay you well."

"I wouldn't do it for pay—not the kind you mean," continued the young inventor.

"What do you mean then?" and Andy's face, that had lighted up, became glum again.

"Well, if I fix your boat for you, will you let me run it a little while?"

"You mean show me how to run it?"

"No, I mean take it myself. Look here, Andy, my boat's been stolen, and I thought you took it to get even with me. You say you didn't——"

"And I didn't touch it," interposed the squint-eyed lad quickly.

"All right, I believe you. But somebody stole it, and I think I know who."

"Who?" asked Sam Snedecker.

"Well, you wouldn't know if I told you, but I suspect some men with whom I had trouble before," and Tom referred to Happy Harry and his gang. "I think they have my boat on this lake, and I'd like to get another speedy craft to cruise about it and make a further search. How about it, Andy? If I fix your boat, will you let me take it to look for my boat?"

"Sure thing!" agreed the bully quickly, and his voice for once was friendly toward Tom. "Fix the engine so it will run, and you can use the *Red Streak* as long as you like."

"Oh, I probably wouldn't want it very long. I could cover the lake in about three days, and I hope by that time I could locate the thieves. Is it a bargain?"

"Sure," agreed Andy again, and Tom got into the motor-boat to look at the engine. He found that it would require some time to adjust it properly and that it would be necessary to take the motor apart.

"I think I'd better tow you to my dock," the young inventor said to Andy. "I can use some tools from the shop then, and by to-night I'll have the *Red Streak* in running order."

The breeze was in the right quarter, fortunately, and with the motor-boat dragging behind, the *Arrow's* owner put the nose of the sailing craft toward his home dock.

When Tom reached his house he found that Mrs. Baggert had received another telephone message from Mr. Swift, inquiring why his son had not returned to Sandport.

"He says if you don't come back by to-morrow," repeated the housekeeper, "that he'll come home by train. He's getting anxious, I believe."

"Shouldn't wonder," admitted Tom. "But I want him to stay there. The change will do him good. I'll soon have my boat back, now that I can go about the lake swiftly, and then I'll join him. I'll tell him to be patient."

Tom talked with his father at some length, assuring him that everything was well at the Shopton house and promising to soon be with him. Then the young inventor began work on the motor of the *Red Streak*. He found it quite a job and had to call on Mr. Jackson to help him, for one of the pistons had to be repaired and a number of adjustments made to the cylinders.

But that night the motor was fully mended and placed back in the boat. It was in better shape than it had been since Andy had purchased the craft.

"There," remarked Tom, "now I'm ready to hunt for those scoundrels. Will you leave your boat at my dock to-night, Andy?"

"Yes, so you can start out early in the morning. I'm not going."

"Why not?" demanded Tom quickly.

"Well—er—you see I've had enough of motoring for a while," explained Andy. "Besides, I don't believe my mother would like me to go out on a chase after thieves. If we had to shoot I might hit one of them, and——"

"Oh, I see," answered Tom. "But I don't like to take your boat alone. Besides, I don't fancy there will be much shooting. I know I'm not going to take a gun. In fact, the one Mr. Duncan gave me is in the boat. All I want is to get the *Arrow* back."

"That's all right," went on Andy. "You take my boat and use it as long as you like. I'll rest up a few days. When you find your boat you can bring mine back."

Tom understood. He was just as glad not to

have Andy accompany him in the chase, as he
and the red-haired lad had never been good
friends and probably never would be. So it would
cause some embarrassment to be together in a
boat all day. Then again Tom knew he could
manage the *Red Streak* better alone, but, of
course, he did not want to mention this when he
asked for the loan of the craft. Andy's own
suggestion, however, had solved the difficulty.
Tom had an idea that Andy felt a little timid
about going in pursuit of the thieves, but naturally
it would not do to mention this, for the squint-
eyed lad considered himself quite a fighter.

Early the next morning, alone in the *Red
Streak,* Tom continued the search for his stolen
boat. He started out from his home dock and
mapped out a course that would take him well
around the lake.

"I s'pose I could take a run to Sandport now,"
mused the youth as he shot in and out of the
little bays, keeping watch for the *Arrow*. "But if
I do dad will have to be told all about it, and he'll
worry. Then, too, he might want to accompany
me, and I think I can manage this better alone,
for the *Red Streak* will run faster with only one
in. I ought to wind up this search in two days,
if my boat is still on the lake. And if those

scoundrels have sunk her I'll make them pay for it."

On shot the speedy motor boat, in and out along the winding shore line, with the lad in the bow at the steering-wheel peering with eager eyes into every nook and corner where his craft might be hidden.

CHAPTER XVII

"THERE SHE IS!"

ANTICIPATING that he would be some time on his search, the young inventor had gone prepared for it. He had a supply of provisions and he had told Mrs. Baggert he might not be back that night. But he did not intend to sleep aboard the *Red Streak,* which, being a racing boat, was not large enough to afford much room for passengers. Tom had planned, therefore, to put up at some hotel near the lake in case his hunt should last beyond one night.

That it would do this was almost certain, for all that morning he searched unavailingly for the *Arrow.* A distant mill whistle sounding over Lake Carlopa told him it was noon.

Dinner time," he announced to himself. "Guess I'll run up along shore in the shade and eat."

Selecting a place where the trees overhung the water, forming a quiet, cool nook, Tom sent the boat in there, and, tying it to a leaning tree, he began his simple meal. Various thoughts filled his mind, but chief among them was the desire to overtake the thieves who had his boat. That it was Happy Harry's gang he was positive.

The lad nearly finished eating and was consid·ering what direction he might best search in next when he heard, running along a road that bordered the lake, an automobile.

"Wonder who that it?" mused Tom. "It won't do any harm to take a look, for it might be some of those thieves again. They probably still have their auto or Happy Harry couldn't have gotten from Sandport to Shopton so quickly."

The young inventor slipped ashore from the motor-boat, taking care to make no noise. Stealing silently along toward the road, he peered through the underbrush for a sight of the machine, which seemed to be going slowly. But before the youth had a glimpse of it he was made aware who the occupant was by hearing some one exclaim:

"Bless my shoe laces if this cantankerous contraption isn't going wrong again! I wonder if it's going to have a fit here in this lonely place. It acts just as if it was. Bless my very existence! Hold on now. Be nice! be nice!"

"Mr. Damon!" exclaimed Tom, and, without knowing it, he had spoken aloud.

"Hold on there! Hold on! Who's calling me in this forsaken locality? Bless my shirt studs! But who is it?" and the eccentric man who had sold Tom the motor-cycle looked intently at the bushes.

"Here I am, Mr. Damon," answered the lad, stepping out into the road. "I knew it was you as soon as I saw you."

"Bless my liver, but that's very true! I suppose you heard my unfortunate automobile puffing along. I declare I don't know what ails it. I got it on the advice of my physician, who said I must get out in the air, but, bless my gears, it's the auto who needs a doctor more than I do! It's continually out of order. Something is going to happen right away. I can tell by the way it's behaving."

Mr. Damon had thrown out the clutch, but the engine was still running, though in a jerky, uncertain fashion which indicated to the trained ear of the young inventor that something was wrong.

"Perhaps I can fix it for you as I did before," ventured Tom.

"Bless my eyebrows! Perhaps you can," cried the eccentric man hopefully. "You always seem to turn up at the right moment. How do you manage it?"

"I don't know. I remember the time you

turned up just when I wanted you to help me capture Happy Harry and his gang, and now, by a strange coincidence, I'm after them again."

"You don't say so! My good gracious! Bless my hatband! But that's odd. There!" he ejaculated suddenly as the automobile engine stopped with a choking sigh, "I knew something was going to happen."

"Let me take a look," proposed the lad, and he was soon busy peering into the interior of the machine. At first he could not find the trouble, but being a persistent youth, Tom went at it systematically and located it in two places. The clutch was not rightly adjusted and the carburetor float feed needed fixing.

The young inventor was not long in making the slight repairs and then he assured Mr. Damon that his automobile would run properly.

"Bless my very existence, but what a thing it is to have a head for mechanics!" exclaimed the odd man gratefully. "Now it would bother me to adjust a nutmeg grater if it got out of order, but I dare say you could fix it in no time."

"Yes," answered Tom, "I could and so could you, for there's nothing about it to fix. But you can go ahead now if you wish."

"Thank you. It just shows how ignorant I am of machinery. I presume something will go wrong in another mile or two. But may I ask what you are doing here? I presume you are in your motor-boat, sailing about for pleasure. And didn't I understand you to say you were after those chaps again? Bless my watch charm, but I was so interested in my machine that I didn't think to ask you."

"Yes, I am after those thieves again."

"In your motor-boat, I presume. Well, I hope you catch them. What have they stolen now?"

"My motor-boat. That's why I'm after them, but I had to borrow a craft to chase them with."

"Bless my soul! You don't tell me! How did it happen?"

Thereupon the lad related as much of the story as was necessary to put Mr. Damon in possession of the facts and he ended up with:

"I don't suppose you have seen anything of the men in my boat, have you?"

Mr. Damon seemed strangely excited. He had entered his auto, but as the lad's story progressed the odd gentleman had descended. When Tom finished he exclaimed:

"Don't say a word now—not a word. I want to think, and that is a process which, for me, requires a little time. Don't speak a word now. Bless my left hand, but I think I can help you!"

He frowned, stamped first one foot, then the

other, looked up at the sky, as if seeking inspiration there, and then down at the ground, as if that would help him to think. Then he clapped his hands smartly together and cried out:

"Bless my shoe buttons!"

"Have you seen them?" asked Tom eagerly.

"Was your boat one with a red arrow painted on the bow?" asked Mr. Damon in turn.

"It was!" and the lad was now almost as excited as was his friend.

"Then I've seen it, and, what's more, this morning! Bless my spark plug, I've seen it!"

"Tell me about it!" pleaded the young inventor, and Mr. Damon, calming himself after an effort, resumed:

"I was out for an early spin in my auto," he said, "and was traveling along a road that bordered the lake, about fifteen miles above here. I heard a motor-boat puffing along near shore, and, looking through the trees, I saw one containing three men. It had a red arrow on the bow, and that's why I noticed it, because I recalled that your boat was named the *Dart*."

"*Arrow*," corrected Tom.

"The *Arrow*. Oh, yes, I knew it was something like that. Well, of course at the time I didn't think that it was your boat, but I associted it in my mind with yours. Do you catch my meaning?"

Tom did and said so, wishing Mr. Damon would hurry and get to the point. But the eccentric character had to do things in his own way.

"Exactly," he resumed. "Well, I didn't think that was your boat, but, at the same time, I watched the men out of curiosity, and I was struck with their behavior. They seemed to be quarreling, and, from what I could hear, two of them seemed to be remonstrating with the third one for having taken some sort of a piece of wood from the forward compartment. I believe that is the proper term."

"Yes!" Tom almost shouted. "But where did they go? What became of them? What was the man doing to the forward compartment—where the gasoline tank is?"

"Exactly. I was trying to think what was kept there. That's it, the gasoline tank. Well, the boat kept on up the lake, and I don't know what became of the men. But about that piece of wood. It seems that one of the men removed a block from under the tank and the others objected. That's why they were quarreling."

"That's very strange," exclaimed the lad. "There must be some mystery about my boat that I don't understand. But that will keep until I get the boat itself. Good-by, Mr. Damon. I must be off."

"Where to?"

"Up the lake after those thieves. I must lose no time,' 'and Tom started to go back to where he had left the *Red Streak*.

"Hold on!" cried Mr. Damon. "I have something to propose, Tom. Two heads are better than one, even if one doesn't know how to adjust a nutmeg grate. Suppose I come along with you? I can point out the direction the men took, at any rate."

"I'll be very glad to have you," answered the lad, who felt that he might need help if there were three of the thieves in his craft. "But what will you do with your automobile?"

"I'll just run it down the road a way to where a friend of mine has a stable. I'll leave it in there and join you. Will you let me come? Bless my eye glasses, but I'd like to help catch those scoundrels!"

"I'll be very glad to have you. Go ahead, put the auto in the barn and I'll wait for you."

"I have a better plan than that," replied Mr. Damon. "Run your boat down to that point," and he indicated one about a mile up the lake. "I'll be there waiting for you, and we'll lose no time. I can cover the ground faster in my auto than you can in your boat."

Tom saw the advantage of this and was soon under way, while he heard on shore the puffing of his friend's car. On the trip to the point Tom puzzled over the strange actions of the man in taking one of the braces from under the gasoline tank.

"I'll wager he did it before," thought the lad. "It must be the same person who was tampering with the lock of the forward compartment the day I bought the boat. But why—that's the question—why?"

He could find no answer to this, puzzle over it as he did, and he gave it up. His whole desire now was to get on the trail of the thieves, and he had strong hopes, after the clew Mr. Damon had given him. The latter was waiting for him on the point, and so nimble was the owner of the auto, in spite of his size, that Tom was not delayed more than the fraction of a minute ere he was under way again, speeding up the lake.

"Now keep well in toward shore," advised Mr. Damon. "Those fellows don't want to be observed any more than they can help, and they'll sneak along the bank. They were headed in that direction," and he pointed it out. "Now I hope you won't think I'm in the way. Besides, you know, if you get your boat back, you'll want some one to help steer it, while you run this one. I can do that, at all events, bless my very existence!"

"I am very glad of your help," replied the lad, but he did not take his eyes from the water before him, and he was looking for a sight of his boat with the men in it.

For three hours or more Tom and Mr. Damon cruised in and out along the shore of the lake, going farther and farther up the body of water. Tom was beginning to think that he would reach Sandport without catching sight of the thieves, and he was wondering if, after all, he might not better stop off and see his father when, above the puffing of the motor in the *Red Streak,* he heard the put-put of another boat.

"Listen!" cried Mr. Damon, who had heard it at the same time.

Tom nodded.

"They're just ahead of us," whispered his companion.

"If it's them," was the lad's reply.

"Speed up and we'll soon see," suggested Mr. Damon, and Tom shoved the timer over. The *Red Streak* forged ahead. The sound of the other boat came more plainly now. It was beyond a little point of land. The young inventor steered out to get around it and leaned eagerly forward to catch the first glimpse of the unseen craft. Would it prove to be the *Arrow?*

The put-put became louder now. Mr. Damon was standing up, as if that would, in some mysterious way, help. Then suddenly the other boat came into view. Tom saw it in an instant and knew it for the *Arrow*.

"There she is!" he cried.

CHAPTER XVIII

THE PURSUIT

FOR an instant after Tom's exultant cry the men in the boat ahead were not aware that they were being pursued. Then, as the explosions from the motor of the *Red Streak* sounded over the water, they turned to see who was coming up behind them. There was no mistaking the attitude of the young inventor and his companion. They were leaning eagerly forward, as if they could reach out and grasp the criminals who were fleeing before them.

"Put on all the speed you can, Tom!" begged Mr. Damon. "We'll catch the scoundrels now. Speed up the motor! Oh, if I only had my automobile now. "Bless my crank shaft, but one can go so much faster on land than on water."

The lad did not reply, but thought, with grim humor, that running an automobile over Lake Carlopa would be no small feat. Mr. Damon, however, knew what he was saying.

"We'll catch them! We'll nab 'em!" he cried. "Speed her up, Tom."

The youth was doing his best with the motor of the *Red Streak*. He was not as well acquainted with it as he was with the one in his boat, but he knew, even better than Andy Foger, how to make it do efficient work. It a foregone conclusion that the *Red Streak*, if rightly handled, could beat the *Arrow*, but there were several points in favor of the thieves. The motor of Tom's boat was in perfect order, and even an amateur, with some knowledge of a boat, could make it do nearly its best. On the other hand, the *Red Streak's* machinery needed "nursing." Again, the thieves had a good start, and that counted for much. But Tom counted on two other points. One was that Happy Harry and his gang would probably know little about the fine points of a motor. They had shown this in letting the motor of the boat they had first stolen get out of order, and Tom knew the ins and outs of a gasoline engine to perfection. So the chase was not so hopeless as it seemed.

"Do you think you can catch them?" asked Mr. Damon anxiously.

"I'm going to make a big try," answered his companion.

"They're heading out into the middle of the lake!" cried the eccentric man.

"If they do, I can cut them off!" murmured Tom as he put the wheel over.

But whoever was steering the *Arrow* knew better than to send it on a course that would enable the pursuing boat to cut across and shorten the distance to it. After sending the stolen craft far enough out from shore to clear points of land that jutted out into the lake, the leading boat was sent straight ahead.

"A stern chase and a long chase!" murmured Mr. Damon. "Bless my rudder, but those fellows are not going to give up easily."

"I guess not," murmured Tom. "Will you steer for a while, Mr. Damon?"

"Of course I will. If I could get out and pull the boat after me, to make it go faster, I would. But as I always lose my breath when I run, perhaps it's just as well that I stay in here."

Tom thought so too, but his attention was soon given to the engine. He adjusted the timer to get if possible a little more speed out of the boat he had borrowed from Andy, and he paid particular attention to the oiling system.

"We're going a bit faster!" called Mr. Damon encouragingly, "or else they're slacking up."

Tom peered ahead to see if this was so. It was hard to judge whether he was overhauling the *Arrow*, as it was a stern chase, and that is always difficult to judge. But a glimpse along shore showed him that they were slipping through the water at a faster speed.

"They're up to something!" suddenly exclaimed Mr. Damon a moment later. "I believe they're going to fire on us, Tom. They are pointing something this way."

The lad stood up and gazed earnestly at his boat, which seemed to be slipping away from him so fast. One of the occupants was in the stern, aiming some glittering object at those in the *Red Streak*. For a moment Tom thought it might be a gun. Then, as the man turned, he saw what it was.

"A pair of marine glasses!" cried the lad. "They're trying to make out who we are."

"I guess they know well enough," rejoined Mr. Damon. "Can't you go any faster, Tom?"

"I'm afraid not. But we'll land them, sooner or later. They can't go very far in this direction without running ashore and we'll have them. They're cutting across the lake now."

"They may escape us if it gets dark. Probably that's what they're working for. They want to keep ahead of us until nightfall."

The young inventor thought of this too, but there was little he could do. The motor was running at top speed. It could be made to go faster,

Tom knew, with another ignition system, but that was out of the question now.

The man with the glasses had resumed his seat, and the efforts of the trio seemed concentrated on the motor of the *Arrow*. They, too, wished to go faster. But they had not skill enough to accomplish it, and in about ten minutes, when Tom took another long and careful look to ascertain if possible whether or not he was overhauling the thieves, he was delighted to see that the distance between the boats had lessened.

"We're catching them! We're creeping up on them!" cried Mr. Damon. "Keep it up, Tom."

There was nothing to do, however, save wait. The boat ahead had shifted her course somewhat and was now turning in toward the shore, for the lake was narrow at this point, and abandoning their evident intention of keeping straight up the lake, the thieves seemed no bent on something else.

"I believe they're going to run ashore and get out!" cried Mr. Damon.

"If they do, it's just what I want," declared the lad. "I don't care for the men. I want my boat back!"

The occupants of the *Arrow* were looking to the rear again, and one—Happy Harry, Tom thought—shook his fist.

"Ah, wait until I get hold of you!" cried Mr. Damon, following his example. "I'll make you wish you'd behaved yourselves, you scoundrels! Bless my overcoat! Catch them if you can, Tom."

There was now no doubt of the intention of the fleeing ones. The shore was looming up ahead and straight for it was headed the *Arrow*. Tom sent Andy's boat in the same direction. He was rapidly overhauling the escaping ones now, for they had slowed down the motor. Three minutes later the foremost boat grated on the beach of the lake. The men leaped out, one of them pausing an instant in the bow.

"Here, don't you damage my boat!" cried Tom involuntarily, for the man seemed to be hammering something.

The fellow leaped over the side, holding something in his hand.

"There they go! Catch them!" yelled Mr. Damon.

"Let them go!" answered the lad as the men ran toward the wood. "I want my boat. I'm afraid they've damaged her. One of them tore something from the bow."

At the same instant the two companions of the fellow who had paused in the forward part of the *Arrow* saw that he had something in his hand. With yells of rage they dashed at him, but he, shaking his fist at them, plunged into the bushes and could be heard breaking his way through, while his companions were in pursuit.

"They've quarreled among themselves," commented Mr. Damon as high and angry voices could be heard from the woods. "There's some mystery here, Tom."

"I don't doubt it, but my first concern is for my boat. I want to see if they have damaged her."

Tom had run so closely in shore with the *Red Streak* that he had to reverse to avoid damaging the craft against the bank. In a mass of foam he stopped her in time, and then springing ashore, he hurried to his motor-boat.

CHAPTER XIX

A QUIET CRUISE

"HAVE they done any damage?" asked Mr. Damon as he stood in the bow of the *Red Streak*.

Tom did not answer for a moment. His trained eye was looking over the engine.

"They yanked out the high tension wire instead of stopping the motor with the switch," he answered at length, and then, when he had taken a look into the compartment where the gasoline tank was, he added: "And they've ripped out two more of the braces I put in. Why in the world they did that I can't imagine."

"That's evidently what one man had that the others wanted," was Mr. Damon's opinion.

"Probably," agreed Tom. "But what could he or they want with wooden braces?"

That was a puzzler for Mr. Damon, but he answered:

"Perhaps they wanted to damage your boat and those two men were mad because the other got ahead of them."

"Taking out the braces wouldn't do much damage. I can easily put others in. All it would do would be to cause the tank to sag down and maybe cause a leak in the pipe. But that would be a queer thing to do. No, I think there's some mystery that I haven't gotten to the bottom of yet. But I'm going to."

"Good!" exclaimed Mr. Damon. "I'll help you. But can you run your boat back home?"

"Not without fixing it a bit. I must brace up that tank and put in a new high tension wire from the spark coil. I can do it here, but I'd rather take it to the shop. Besides, with two boats to run back, for I must return Andy's to him, I don't see how I can do it very well unless you operate one, Mr. Damon."

"Excuse me, but I can't do it. Bless my slippers, but I would be sure to run on a rock! The best plan will be for you to tow your boat and I'll ride in it and steer. I can do that much, anyhow. You can ride in the *Red Streak.*

Tom agreed that this would be a good plan. So, after temporarily bracing up the tank in the *Arrow*, it was shoved out into the lake and attached to Andy's craft.

"But aren't you going to make a search for those men?" asked Mr. Damon when Tom was ready to start back.

"No, I think it would be useless. They are well away by this time, and I don't fancy chasing them through the woods, especially as night is coming on. Besides, I won't leave these boats."

"No doubt you are right, but I would like to see them punished, and I am curious enough to wish to know what object that scoundrel could have in ripping out the blocks that served as a brace for the tank."

"I feel the same way myself," commented the lad, "especially since this is the second time that's happened. But we'll have a wait, I guess."

A little later the start back was made, Mr. Damon steering the *Arrow* skilfully enough so that it did not drag on the leading boat, in which Tom rode. His course took him not far from the lake sanitarium, where Mr. Duncan, the hunter, had been brought, and desiring to know how the wounded man was getting on, the youth proposed that they make a halt, explaining to Mr. Damon his reason.

"Yes, and while you're about it you'd better telephone your father that you will join him to-morrow," suggested the other. "I know what it is to fret and worry. You can fix your boat up in time to go to Sandport to-morrow, can't you?"

"Yes, I'm glad you reminded me of it. I'll telephone from the sanitarium, if they'll let me."

Mr. Duncan was not at the institution, Tom was told, his injury having healed sufficiently to allow of his being removed to his home. The youth readily secured permission to use the telephone, and was soon in communication with Mr. Swift. While not telling him all the occurrences that had delayed him, Tom gave his father and Ned Newton enough information to explain his absence. Then the trip to Shopton was resumed in the two boats.

"What are you going to do about your automobile?" asked Tom as they neared the point where the machine had been left.

"Never mind about that," replied Mr. Damon. "It will do it good to have a night's vacation. I will go on to your house with you, and perhaps I can get a train back to my friend's home, so that I can claim my car."

"Won't you stay all night with me?" invited the young inventor. "I'd be glad to have you."

Mr. Damon agreed, and, Tom putting more speed on the *Red Streak*, was soon opposite his own dock. The *Arrow* was run in the boathouse and the owner hastily told Mrs. Baggert and the engineer what had occurred. Then he took Andy's boat to Mr. Foger's dock and warmly thanked the red-haired lad for the use of his craft.

"Did you find your boat?" asked Andy eagerly. "How did the *Red Streak* run?"

"I got my boat and yours run fine," explained Tom.

"Good! I'll race you again some day," declared Andy.

Mr. Damon enjoyed his visit at our hero's house, for Mrs. Baggert cooked one of her best suppers for him. Tom and the engineer spent the evening repairing the motor-boat, Mr. Damon looking on and exclaiming "Bless my shoe leather" or some other part of his dress or anatomy at every stage of the work. The engineer wanted to know all about the men and their doings, but he could supply no reason for their queer actions regarding the braces under the gasoline tank.

In the morning Tom once more prepared for an early start for Sandport, and Mr. Damon, reconsidering his plans, rode as far with him as the place where the automobile had been left. There he took leave of the young inventor, promising to call on Mr. Swift in the near future.

"I hope you arrive at the hotel where your father is without any more accidents," remarked the automobilist. "Bless my very existence, but you seem to have the most remarkable series of adventures I ever heard of!"

"They are rather odd," admitted Tom. "I don't know that I particularly care for them, either. But, now that I have my boat back, I guess everything will be all right."

But Tom could not look ahead. He was destined to have still more exciting times, as presently will be related.

Without further incident he arrived at the Lakeview Hotel in Sandport that evening and found his father and Ned very glad to see him. Of course he had to explain everything then, and, with his son safely in his sight, Mr. Swift was not so nervous over the recital as he would have been had Tom not been present.

"Now for some nice, quiet trips," remarked the lad when he had finished his account. "I feel as if I had cheated you out of part of your vacation, Ned, staying away as long as I did."

"Well, of course we missed you," answered his chum. "But your father and I had a good time."

"Yes, and I invented a new attachment for a kitchen boiler," added Mr. Swift. "I had a chance for it when I passed through the hotel kitchen one day, for I wanted to see what kind of a range they used."

"I guess there's no stopping you from inventing," replied his son with a laugh and a hopeless shake of the head. "But don't let it happen again when you go away to rest."

"Oh, I only just thought of it," said Mr. Swift. "I haven't worked the details out yet."

Then he wanted to know about everything at home and he seemed particularly anxious lest the Happy Harry gang do some damage.

"I don't believe they will," Tom assured him. "Garret and Mrs. Baggert will be on guard."

The next few days were pleasant ones for Tom, his father and Ned Newton. They cruised about the lake, went fishing and camped in the woods. Even Mr. Swift spent one night in the tent and said he liked it very much. For a week the three led an ideal existence, doing about as they pleased, Ned taking a number of photographs with his new camera. The *Arrow* proved herself a fine boat, and Tom and Ned, when Mr. Swift did not accompany them, explored the seldom visited parts of Lake Carlopa.

The three had been out one day and were discussing the necessity of returning home soon when Ned spoke.

"I shall hate to give up this life and go to slaving in the bank again," he complained. "I wish I was an inventor."

"Oh, we inventors don't have such an easy time," said Mr. Swift. "You never know when trouble is coming," and he little imagined how near the truth he was.

A little later they were at the hotel dock. When Tom had tied up his boat the three walked up the path to the broad veranda that faced the lake. A boy in uniform met them.

"Some one has just called you on the telephone, Mr. Swift," he reported.

"Some one wants me? Who is it?"

"I think he said his name is Jackson, sir, Garret Jackson, and he says the message is very important."

"Tom, something has happened at home!" exclaimed the inventor as he hurried up the steps. "I'm afraid there's bad news."

Unable to still the fear in his heart, Tom followed his father.

CHAPTER XX

NEWS OF A ROBBERY

WITH a hand that trembled so he could scarcely hold the receiver of the telephone, Mr. Swift placed it to his ear.

"Hello! hello!" he cried into the transmitter. "Yes, this is Mr. Swift—yes, Garret. What is it?"

Then came a series of clicks, which Tom and Ned listened to. The inventor spoke again.

"What's that! The same men? Broke in early this evening? Oh, that's too bad! Of course, I'll come at once."

There followed more meaningless clicks, which Tom wished he could translate. His father hung up the receiver, turned to him and exclaimed:

"I've been robbed again!"

"Robbed again! How, dad?"

"By that same rascally gang, Garret thinks. This evening, when he and Mrs. Baggert were in the house the burglar alarm went off. The indi cator showed that the electrical shop had been entered, and the engineer hurried there. He saw a light inside and the shadows of persons on the windows. Before he could reach the shop, however, the thieves heard him coming and escaped. Oh, Tom, I should never have come away!"

"But did they take anything, dad? Perhaps Garret frightened them away before they had a chance to steal any of your things. Did you ask him that?"

"I didn't need to. He said he made a hasty examination before he called me up, and he is sure a number of my electrical inventions are missing. Some of them are devices I never have had patented, and if I lose them I will have no recovery."

"But just what ones are they? Perhaps we can send out a police alarm to-night."

"Garret couldn't tell that," answered Mr. Swift as he paced to and fro in the hotel office. "He doesn't know all the tools and machinery I had in there. But it is certain that some of my most valuable things have been taken."

"Never mind. Don't worry, dad," and Tom tried to speak soothingly, for he saw that his father was much excited. "We may be able to get them back. How does Garret know the same men who stole the turbine model broke in the shop this evening?"

"He saw them. One was Happy Harry, he is positive. The others he did not know, but he recognized the tramp from our description of him."

"Then we must tell the police at once."

"Yes, Tom, I wish you would telephone. I'll give you a description of the things. No, I can't do that either, for I don't know what was stolen. I must go home at once to find out. It's a good thing the motor-boat is here. Come, let's start at once. What is my bill here?" and the inventor turned to the hotel proprietor, who had come into the office. "I have suffered a severe loss and must leave at once."

"I am very sorry, sir. I'll have it ready for you in a few minutes."

"All right. Tom, is you boat ready for a quick trip?"

"Yes, dad, but I don't like to make it at night with three in. Of course it might be perfectly safe, but there's a risk, and I don't like to take it."

"Don't worry about the risk on my account, Tom. I'm not afraid. I must get home and see of what I have been robbed."

The young inventor was in a quandary. He wanted to do as his father requested and to aid him all he could, yet he knew that an all-night trip in the boat down the lake would be dangerous, not only from the chance of running on an unknown shore or into a hidden rock, but because Mr. Swift was not physically fitted to stand the journey.

"Come, Tom," exclaimed the aged inventor impatiently, "we must start at once!"

"Won't morning do as well, dad?"

"No, I must start now. I could not sleep worrying over what has happened. We will start——"

At that instant there came a low, rumbling peal of thunder. Mr. Swift started and peered from a window. There came a flash of lightning and another vibrant report from the storm-charged clouds.

"There is your bill, Mr. Swift," remarked the proprietor, coming up, "but I would not advise you to start to-night. There is a bad storm in the west, and it will reach here in a few minutes. Storms on Lake Carlopa, especially at this open and exposed end, are not to be despised, I assure you."

"But I *must* get home!" insisted Tom's father.

The lace curtain over the window blew almost straight out with a sudden breeze, and a flash of lightning so bright that it reflected even in the room where the incandescent electrics were glowing made several others jump. Then came a

mighty crash, and with that the flood-gates of the
storm were opened, and the rain came down in
torrents. Tom actually breathed a sigh of relief.
The problem was solved for him. It would be impossible to start to-night, and he was glad of it,
much as he wanted to get on the trail of the
thieves.

There was a scurrying on the part of the hotel
attendants to close the windows, and the guests
who had been enjoying the air out on the porches
came running in. With a rush, a roar and a mut-
tering, as peal after peal of thunder sounded, the
deluge continued.

"It's a good thing we didn't start," observed
Ned.

"I should say so," agreed Tom. "But we'll
get off the first thing in the morning, dad."

Mr. Swift did not reply, but his nervous pacing
to and fro in the hotel office showed how anxious
he was to be at home again. There was no help
for it, however, and, after a time, finding that to
think of reaching his house that night was out of
the question, the inventor calmed down somewhat

The storm continued nearly all night, as Tom
could bear witness, for he did not sleep well, nor
did his father. And when he came down to breakfast in the morning Mr. Swift plainly showed the
effects of the bad news. His face was haggard

and drawn and his eyes smarted and burned from lack of sleep.

"Well, Tom, we must start early," he said nervously. "I am glad it has cleared off. Is the boat all ready?"

"Yes, and it's a good thing it was under shelter last night or we'd have to bail it out now, and that would delay us."

An hour later they were under way, having telephoned to the engineer at the Swift home that they were coming. Garret Jackson reported over the wire that he had notified the Shopton police of the robbery, but that little could be done until the inventor arrived to give a description of the stolen articles.

"And that will do little good, I fear," remarked Tom. "Those fellows have evidently been planning this for some time and will cover their tracks well. I'd like to catch them, not only to recover your things, dad, but to find out the mystery of my boat and why the man took the tank braces."

CHAPTER XXI

THE BALLOON ON FIRE

Down Lake Carlopa speeded the *Arrow*, those on board watching the banks slip past as the motor-boat rapidly cut through the water.

"What time do you think we ought to reach home, Tom?" 'asked Mr. Swift.

"Oh, about four o'clock, if we don't stop for lunch."

"Then we'll not stop," decided the inventor. "We'll eat what we have on board. I suppose you have some rations?" and he smiled, the first time since hearing the bad news.

"Oh, yes, Ned and I didn't eat everything on our camping trips," and Tom was glad to note that the fine weather which followed the storm was having a good effect on his father.

"We certainly had a good time," remarked Ned. "I don't know when I've enjoyed a vacation so."

"It's too bad it had to be cut short by this robbery," commented Mr. Swift.

"Oh, well, my time would be up in a few days more," went on the young bank employé. "It's just as well to start back now."

Tom took the shortest route he knew, keeping in as close to shore as he dared, for now he was as anxious to get home as was his father. On and on speeded the *Arrow,* yet fast as it was, it seemed slow to Mr. Swift, who, like all nervous persons, always wanted to go wherever he desired to go instantly.

Tom headed his boat around a little point of land, and was urging the engine to the top notch of speed, for now he was on a clear course, with no danger from shoals or hidden rocks, when he saw, darting out from shore, a tiny craft which somehow seemed familiar to him. He recognized a peculiar put-putter of the motor.

"That's the *Dot,*" he remarked in a low voice to Ned, "Miss Nestor's cousin's boat."

"Is she in it now?" asked Ned.

"Yes," answered Tom quickly.

"You've got good eyesight," remarked Ned drÿly, "to tell a girl at that distance. It looks to me like a boy."

"No, it's Mary—I mean Miss Nestor," the youth quickly corrected himself, and a close observer would have noticed that he blushed a bit under his coat of tan.

Ned laughed, Tom blushed still more, and Mr. Swift, who was in a stern seat, glanced up quickly.

"It looks as if that boat wanted to hail us," the inventor remarked.

Tom was thinking the same thing, for, though he had changed his course slightly since sighting the *Dot*, the little craft was put over so as to meet him. Wondering what Miss Nestor could want, but being only too willing to have a chat with her, the young inventor shifted his helm. In a short time the two craft were within hailing distance.

"How do you do?" called Miss Nestor, as she slowed down her motor. "Don't you think I'm improving, Mr. Swift?"

"What's that? I—er—I beg your pardon. but I didn't catch that," exclaimed the aged inventor quickly, coming out of a sort of day-dream. "I beg your pardon." He thought she had addressed him.

Miss Nestor blushed and looked questioningly at Tom.

"My father," he explained as he introduced his parent. Ned needed none, having met Miss Nestor before. "Indeed you have improved very much," went on our hero. "You seem able to manage the boat all alone."

"Yes, I'm doing pretty well. Dick lets me take the *Dot* whenever I want to, and I thought I'd come out for a little trial run this morning. I'm getting ready for the races. I suppose you are going to enter them?" and she steered her boat alongside Tom's, who throttled down his powerful motor so as not to pass his friend.

"Races? I hadn't heard of them," he replied.

"Oh, indeed there are to be fine ones under the auspices of the Lanton Motor Club. Mr. Hastings, of whom you bought that boat, is going to enter his new *Carlopa,* and Dick has entered the *Dot,* in the baby class of course. But I'm going to run it, and that's why I'm practicing."

"I hope you win," remarked Tom. "I hadn't heard of the races, but I think I'll enter. I'm glad you told me. Do you want to race now?" and he laughed as he looked into the brown eyes of Mary Nestor.

"No, indeed, unless you give me a start of several miles."

They kept together for some little time longer, and then, as Tom knew his father would be restless at the slow speed, he told Miss Nestor the need of haste, and, advancing his timer, he soon left the *Dot* behind. The girl called a laughing good-by and urged him not to forget the races, which were to take place in about two weeks.

"I suppose Andy Foger will enter his boat," commented Ned.

"Naturally," agreed Tom. "It's a racer, and he'll probably think it can beat anything on the lake. But if he doesn't manage his motor differently, it won't."

The distance from Sandport to Shopton had been more than half covered at noon, when the travelers ate a lunch in the boat. Mr. Swift was looking anxiously ahead to catch the first glimpse of his dock and Tom was adjusting the machinery as finely as he dared to get out of it the maximum speed.

Ned Newton, who happened to be gazing aloft, wondering at the perfect beauty of the blue sky after the storm, uttered a sudden exclamation. Then he arose and pointed at some object in the air.

"Look!" he cried, "a balloon! It must have gone up from some fair."

Tom and his father looked upward. High in the air, almost over their heads, was an immense balloon. It was of the hot-air variety, such as performers use in which to make ascensions from fair grounds and circuses, and below it dangled a trapeze, upon which could be observed a man, only he looked more like a doll than a human being.

"I shouldn't like to be as high as that," remarked Ned.

"I would," answered Tom as he slowed down

the engine the better to watch the balloon. "I'd like to go up in an airship, and I intend to some day."

"I believe he's going to jump!" suddenly exclaimed Ned after a few minutes. "He's going to do something, anyhow."

"Probably come down in a parachute," said Tom. "They generally do that."

"No! no!" cried Ned. "He isn't going to jump. Something has happened! The balloon is on fire! He'll be burned to death!"

Horror stricken, they all gazed aloft. From the mouth of the balloon there shot a tongue of fire, and it was followed by a cloud of black smoke. The big bag was getting smaller and seemed to be descending, while the man on the trapeze was hanging downward by his hands to get as far as possible away from the terrible heat.

CHAPTER XXII

THE RESCUE

"JUMP! jump!" cried Mr. Swift, leaping to his feet and motioning to the man on the trapeze of the balloon. But it is doubtful whether or not the performer heard him. Certainly he could not see the frantic motions of the inventor. "Why doesn't he jump?" Mr. Swift went on piteously to the two lads. "He'll surely be burned to death if he hangs on there!"

"It's too far to leap!" exclaimed Tom. "He's a good way up in the air, though it looks like only a short distance. He would be killed if he dropped now."

"He ought to have a parachute," added Ned. "Most of those men do when they go up in a balloon. Why doesn't he come down in that? I wonder how the balloon took fire?"

"Maybe he hasn't a parachute," suggested Tom, while he slowed down the motor-boat still more so as to remain very nearly under the blazing balloon.

"Yes, he has!" cried Ned. "See, it's hanging to one side of the big bag. He ought to cut loose. He could save himself then. Why doesn't he?"

The balloon was slowly twisting about, gradually settling to the surface of the lake, but all the while the flames were becoming fiercer and the black clouds of smoke increased in size.

"There, see the parachute!" went on Ned.

The twisting of the bag had brought into view the parachute or big, umbrella-shaped bag, which would have enabled the man to safely drop to the surface of the lake. Without it he would have hit the water with such force that he would have been killed as surely as if he had struck the solid earth. But the boys and Mr. Swift also saw something else, and this was that the balloon was on fire on the same side where the parachute was suspended.

"Look! look!" shouted Tom, bringing his boat to a stop. "That's why he can't jump! He can't reach the parachute!"

By this time the balloon had settled so low that the actions of the man could be plainly seen. That he was in great agony of fear, as well as in great pain from the terrific heat over his head was evident. He shifted about on the trapeze bar, now hanging by one hand, so as to bring his body a little farther below the blazing end of the bag, then, when one arm tired, he would hang by the other. If the balloon would only come down more quickly it would get to within such a short distance of the water that the man could safely make the drop.

But the immense canvas bag was settling so slowly, for it was still very buoyant, that considerable time must elapse before it would be near enough to the water to make it safe for the unfortunate man to let go the trapeze.

"Oh, if we could only do something!" cried Tom. "We have to remain here helpless and watch him burn to death. It's awful!"

The three in the boat continued to gaze upward. They could see the man making frantic efforts to reach his parachute from time to time. Once, as a little current of air blew the flames and smoke to one side, he thought he had a chance. Up on the trapeze bar he pulled himself and then edged along it in an endeavor to grasp the ring of the parachute. Once he almost had hold of that and also the cord, which ran to a knife blade. This cord, being pulled, would sever the rope that bound it to the balloon, and he would be comparatively safe, so he might drop to the lake. But, just as he was about to grasp the ring and cord, the smoke came swirling down on him and the hungry flames seemed to put out their fiery tongues to devour him. He had to slide back and once more hung by his hands.

"I thought he was saved then," whispered Tom, and even the whisper sounded loud in the silence.

Several men came running along the shore of the lake now. They saw the occupants in the *Arrow* and cried out:

"Why don't you save him? Go to his rescue!"

"What can we do?" asked Ned quietly of his two friends, but he did not trouble to answer the men on shore, who probably did not know what they were saying.

The motor-boat had drifted from a spot under the unfortunate balloonist, and at a word from his father the young inventor started the engine and steered the craft back directly under the blazing bag again.

"If he does drop, perhaps we may be able to pick him up," said Mr. Swift. "I wish we could save him!"

A cry from Ned startled Tom and his father, and their eyes, that had momentarily been directed away from the burning bag high in the air, were again turned toward it.

"The balloon is falling apart!" exclaimed Ned. "It's all up with him now!"

Indeed it did seem so, for pieces of the burning canvas, blazing and smoking, were falling in a shower from the part of the bag already consumed, and the fiery particles were fairly raining down on the man. But he still had his wits about him, though his perilous position was enough to make any one lose his mind, and he swung from side to side on the bar, shifting skilfully with his hands and dodging the larger particles of blazing canvas. When some small sparks fell on his clothing he beat them out with one hand, while with the other he clung to the trapeze.

There was scarcely any wind or the man's plight might have been more bearable, for the current of air would have carried the smoke and fire to one side. As it was, most of the smoke and flames went straight up, save now and then, when a draught created by the heat would swirl the black clouds down on the performer, hiding him from sight for a second or two. A breeze would have carried the sparks away instead of letting them fall on him.

Nearer and nearer to the surface of the lake sank the balloon. By this time the crowd on the bank had increased and there were excited opinions as to what was best to do. But the trouble was that little could be done. If the man could hold out until he got near enough to the water to let go he might yet be saved, but this would not be for some time at the present rate the balloon was falling. The performer realized this, and, as the fire was getting hotter, he made another desperate attempt to reach the parachute. It was unavailing and he had to drop back, hanging below the slender bar.

Suddenly there came a puff of wind, fanning the faces of those in the motor-boat, and they looked intently to observe if there was any current as high as was the balloonist. They saw the big bag sway to one side and the flames broke out more fiercely as they caught the draught. The balloon moved slowly down the lake.

"Keep after it, Tom!" urged his father. "We may be able to save him!"

The lad increased the speed of his engine and Ned, who was at the wheel, gave it a little twist.

Then, with a suddenness that was startling, the blazing canvas airship began to settle swiftly toward the water. It had lost much of its buoyancy.

"Now he can jump! He's near enough to the water now!" cried Tom.

But a new danger arose. True, the balloon was rapidly approaching the surface of the lake and in a few seconds more would be within such a short distance that a leap would not be fatal. But the burning bag was coming straight down and scarcely would the man be in the water ere the fiery canvas mass would be on top of him.

In such an event he would either be burned to death or so held down that drowning must quickly follow.

"If there was only wind enough to carry the balloon beyond him after he jumped he could do it safely!" cried Ned.

Tom said nothing. He was measuring, with his eye, the distance the balloon had yet to go and also the distance away the motor-boat was from where it would probably land.

"He can do it!" exclaimed the young inventor.

"How?" asked his father.

For answer Tom caught up a newspaper he had purchased at the hotel that morning. Rolling it quickly into a cone, so that it formed a rough megaphone, he put the smaller end to his mouth, and, pointing the larger opening at the balloonist, he called out:

"Drop into the lake! We'll pick you up before the bag falls on you! Jump! Let go now!"

The balloonist heard and understood. So did Ned and Mr. Swift. Tom's quick wit had found a way to save the man.

Faster and faster the blazing bag settled toward the surface of the water. It was now merely a mushroom-shaped piece of burning and smoking canvas, yet it was supporting the man almost as a parachute would have done.

With one look upward to the burning mass above him and a glance downward to the lake, the aeronaut let go his hold. Like a shot he came down, holding his body rigid and straight as a stick, for he knew how to fall into water, did that balloonist.

Tom Swift was ready for him. No sooner had the lad called his directions through the megaphone than the young inventor had speeded up his engine to the top notch.

"Steer so as to pick him up!" Tom cried to Ned, who was at the wheel. "Pass by him on a curve, and, as soon as I grab him, put the wheel over so as to get out from under the balloon."

It was a risky thing to do, but our hero had it all planned out. He made a loop of the boat's painter, and, hurrying to the bow, leaned over as far as he could, holding the rope in readiness. His idea was to have the balloonist grab the strands and be pulled out of danger by the speedy motor-boat, for the blazing canvas would cover such an extent of water that the man could not have swum out of the danger zone in time.

Down shot the balloonist and down more slowly settled the collapsed bag, yet not so slowly that there was any time to spare. It needed only a few seconds to drop over the performer, to burn and smother him.

Into the water splashed the man, disappearing from sight as when a stick is dropped in, point first. Ned was alert and steered the boat to the side in which the man's face was, for he concluded that the aeronaut would strike out in that direction when he came up. The *Arrow* was now directly under the blazing balloon and cries of fear from the watchers on shore urged upon Tom and his companions the danger of their position. But they had to take some risk to rescue the man.

"There he is!" cried Mr. Swift, who was on the watch, leaning over the side of the boat. Tom and Ned saw him at the same instant. Ned shifted his wheel and the young inventor bent over, holding out the rope for the man to grasp. He saw it and struck out toward the *Arrow*. But there was no need for him to go far. An instant more and the speeding motor-boat shot past him. He grabbed the rope and Tom, aided by Mr. Swift, began to lift him out of the water.

"Quick! To one side, Ned!" yelled Tom, for the heat of the descending mass of burning canvas struck him like a furnace blast.

Ned needed no urging. With a swirl of the screw the *Arrow* shot herself out of the way, carrying the aeronaut with her. A moment later the burning balloon, or what there was left of it, settled down into the lake, hissing angrily as the fire was quenched by the water and completely covering the spot where, but a few seconds before, the man had been swimming. He had been saved in the nick of time.

CHAPTER XXIII

PLANS FOR AN AIRSHIP

"Slow her down, Ned!" cried Tom, for the *Arrow* was shooting so swiftly through the water that the young inventor found it impossible to pull up the balloonist. Ned hurried back to the motor, and, when the boat's way had been checked, it was an easy matter to pull the dripping and almost exhausted man into the craft.

"Are you much hurt?" asked Mr. Swift anxiously, for Tom was too much out of breath with his exertion to ask any questions. For that matter the man was in almost as bad a plight. He was breathing heavily, as one who had run a long race.

"I—I guess I'm all right," he panted. "Only burned a little on my hands. That—that was a close call!"

The boat swung around and headed for shore, on which was quite a throng of persons. Some of them had cheered when they saw the plucky rescue.

"I'm afraid we can't save your balloon," gasped

Tom as he looked at the place where the canvas was still floating and burning.

"No matter. It wasn't worth much. That's the last time I'll ever go up in a hot-air balloon," said the man with more energy than he had before exhibited. "I'm done with 'em. I've had my lesson. Hereafter an aeroplane or a gas balloon for mine. I only did this to oblige the fair committee. I'll not do it again."

The man spoke in short, crisp sentences, as though he was in too much of a hurry to waste his words.

"Let it sink," he went on. "It's no good. Glad to see the last of it."

Almost as he spoke, with a final hiss and a cloud of steam that mingled with the black smoke, the remains of the big bag sunk beneath the surface of the lake.

"We must get you ashore at once and to a doctor," said Mr. Swift. "You must be badly burned."

"Not much. Only my hands, where some burning pieces of canvas fell on 'em. If I had a little oil to put on I'd be all right."

"I can fix you up better than that," put in Tom. "I have some vaseline."

"Good! Just the thing. Pass it over," and the man, though he spoke shortly, seemed grateful for the offer. "My name's Sharp," he went on, "John Sharp, of no place in particular, for I travel all over. I'm a professional balloonist. Ha! that's the stuff!"

This last was in reference to a bottle of vaseline which Tom produced. Mr. Sharp spread some over the backs of his hands and went on:

"That's better. Much obliged. I can't begin to thank you for what you did for me—saved my life. I thought it was all up with me—would have been but for you. Mustn't mind my manner—it's a way I have—have to talk quick when you're balloonin'—no time—but I'm grateful all the same. Who might you people be?"

Tom told him their names and Mr. Swift asked the aeronaut if he was sure he didn't need the services of a physician.

"No doctor for me," answered the balloonist. "I've been in lots of tight places, but this was the worst squeeze. If you'll put me ashore, I guess I can manage now."

"But you're all wet," objected Tom. Where will you go? You need some other clothes," for the man wore a suit of tights and spangles.

"Oh, I'm used to this," went on the performer. "I frequently have to fall in the water. I always carry a little money with me so as to get back to the place where I started from. By the way, where am I?"

"Opposite Daleton," answered Tom. "Where did you go up from?"

"Pratonia. Big fair there. I was one of the features."

"Then you're about fifteen miles away," commented Mr. Swift. "You can hardly get back before night. Must you go there?"

"Left my clothes there. Also a valuable gas balloon. No more hot-air ones for me. Guess I'd better go back, and the aeronaut continued to speak in his quick, jerky sentences.

"We'd be very glad to have you come with us, Mr. Sharp," went on the inventor. "We are not far from Shopton, and if you would like to remain over night I'm sure we would make you comfortable. You can proceed to Pratonia in the morning."

"Thanks. Might not be a bad idea," said Mr. Sharp. "I'm obliged to you. I've got to go there to collect my money, though I suppose they won't give it all to me."

"Why not?" demanded Ned.

"Didn't drop from my parachute. Couldn't. Fire was one reason—couldn't reach the parachute, and if I could have, guess it wouldn't have been safe. Parachute probably was burned too.

But I'm done with hot-air balloons, though I guess I said that before."

The boys were much interested in the somewhat odd performer, and, on his part, he seemed to take quite a notion to Tom, who told him of several things that he had invented.

"Well," remarked Mr. Swift after a while, during which the boat had been moving slowly down the lake, "if we are not to go ashore for a doctor for you, Mr. Sharp, suppose we put on more speed and get to my home? I'm anxious about a robbery that occurred there," and he related some facts in the case.

"Speed her up!" exclaimed Mr. Sharp. "Wish I could help you catch the scoundrels, but afraid I can't—hands too sore," and he looked at his burns. Then he told how he had made the ascension from the Pratonia fair grounds and how, when he was high in the air, he had discovered that the balloon was on fire. He described his sensations and told how he thought his time had surely come. Sparks from the hot air used to inflate it probably caused the blaze, he said.

"I've made a number of trips," he concluded, "hot air and gas bags, but this was the worst ever. It got on my nerves for a few minutes," he added coolly.

"I should think it would," agreed Tom as he

speeded up the motor and sent the *Arrow* on her homeward way.

The boys and Mr. Swift were much interested in the experiences of the balloonist and asked him many questions, which he answered modestly. Several hours passed and late that afternoon the party approached Shopton.

"Here we are!" exclaimed Mr. Swift, relief in his tones. "Now to see of what I have been robbed and to get the police after the scoundrels!"

When the boat was nearing the dock Mr. Sharp, who had been silent for some time, suddenly turned to Tom and asked:

"Ever invent an airship?"

"No," replied the lad, somewhat surprised. "I never did."

"I have," went on the balloonist. "That is, I've invented part of it. I'm stuck over some details. Maybe you and I'll finish it some day. How about it?"

"Maybe," assented Tom, who was occupied just then in making a good landing. "I am interested in airships, but I never thought I could build one."

"Easiest thing in the world," went on Mr. Sharp, as if it was an everyday matter. "You and I will get busy as soon as we clear up this robbery." He talked as though he had been a friend of the family for some time, for he had a genial, taking manner.

A little later Mr. Swift was excitedly questioning Garret Jackson concerning the robbery and making an examination of the electrical shop to discover what was missing.

"The've taken some parts of my gyroscope!" he exclaimed, "and some valuable tools and papers, as well as some unfinished work that will be difficult to replace."

"Much of a loss?" asked Mr. Sharp with a business-like air.

"Well, not so large as regards money," answered the inventor, "but they took things I can never replace, and I will miss them very much if I cannot get them back."

"Then we'll get 'em back!" snapped the balloonist, as if that was all there was to it.

The police were called up on the telephone and the facts given to them, as well as a description of the stolen things. They promised to do what they could, but, in the light of past experiences, Tom and his father did not think this would be much. There was little more that could be done that evening. Ned Newton went to his home, and, after Mr. Swift had insisted in calling in his physician to look after Mr. Sharp's burns, the balloonist was given a room next to Tom's. Then the Swift household settled down.

"Well," remarked Tom to his father as he got ready for bed, "this sure has been an exciting day."

"And my loss is a serious one," added the inventor somewhat sadly.

"Don't worry, dad," begged his son. "I'll do my best to recover those things for you."

Several days passed, but there was no clew to the thieves. That they were the same ones who had stolen the turbine model there was little doubt, but they seemed to have covered their tracks well. The police were at a loss, and, though Tom and Mr. Sharp cruised about the lake, they could get no trace of the men. The balloonist had sent to Pratonia for his clothing and other baggage and was now installed in the Swift home, where he was invited to stay a week or two.

One night when he was looking over some papers he had taken from his trunk the balloonist came over to where Tom was making a drawing of a new machine he was planning and said:

"Like to see my idea for an airship? Different from some. It's a dirigible balloon with an aeroplane front and rear to steer and balance it in big winds. It would be a winner, only for one thing. Maybe you can help me."

"Maybe I can," agreed Tom, who was at once interested.

"We ought to be able to do something. Look at our names—Swift and Sharp—quick and penetrating—a good firm to build airships," and he laughed genially. "Shall we do it?"

"I'm willing," agreed Tom, and the balloonist spread his plans out on the table, he and the young inventor soon being deep in a discussion of them.

CHAPTER XXIV

THE MYSTERY SOLVED

FROM then on, for several days, the young inventor and his new friend lived in an atmosphere of airships. They talked them from morning until night, and even Mr. Swift, much as he was exercised over his loss, took part in the discussions.

In the meanwhile efforts had not ceased to locate the robbers and recover the stolen goods, but so far without success.

One afternoon, about two weeks after the thrilling rescue of John Sharp, Tom said to the balloonist:

"Wouldn't you like to come for a ride in the motor-boat? Maybe it will help us to solve the puzzle of the airship. We'll take a trip across and up the opposite shore."

"Good idea," commented Mr. Sharp. "Fine day for a sail. Come on. Blow the cobwebs from our brains."

Mr. Swift declined an invitation to accompany

them, as he said he would stay home and try to straighten out his affairs, which were somewhat muddled by the robbery.

Out over the blue waters of Lake Carlopa shot the *Arrow*. It was making only moderate speed, as Tom was in no hurry, and he knew his engine would last longer if not forced too frequently. They glided along, crossed the lake and were proceeding up the opposite shore when, as they turned out from a little bay and rounded a point of land, Mr. Sharp exclaimed:

"Look out, Tom, there's rowboat just ahead!"

"Oh, I'll pass well to one side of that," answered the young inventor, looking at the craft. As he did so, noting that there were four men in it, one of the occupants caught a glimpse of the *Arrow*. No sooner had he done so than he spoke to his companions, and they all turned to stare at Tom. At first the lad could scarcely believe his eyes, but as he looked more intently he uttered a cry.

"There they are!"

"Who?" inquired Mr. Sharp.

"Those men—the thieves! We must catch them!"

Tom had spoken loudly, but even though the men in the rowboat did hear what he said, they would have realized without that that they were about to be pursued, for there was no mistaking the attitude of our hero.

Two of the thieves were at the oars, and, with one accord, they at once increased their speed. The boat swung about sharply and was headed for the shore, which they seemed to have come from only a short time previous, as the craft was not far out in the lake.

"No, you don't!" cried Tom. "I see your game! You want to get to the woods, where you'll have a better chance to escape! If this isn't great luck, coming upon them this way!"

It was the work of but a moment to speed up the engine and head the *Arrow* for the rowboat. The men were pulling frantically, but they had no chance.

"Get between them and the shore!" cried Mr. Sharp. "You can head them off then."

This was good advice and Tom followed it. The men, among whom the lad could recognize Happy Harry and Anson Morse, were all excited. Two of them stood up, as though to jump overboard, but their companions called to them to stop.

"If we only had a gun now, not to shoot at them but to intimidate them," murmured the balloonist, "maybe they'd stop."

"Here's one," answered Tom, pointing to the seat locker, where he kept the shotgun Mr. Duncan had given him. In a moment Mr. Sharp had it out.

"Surrender!" he cried, pointing the weapon at the men in the small boat.

"Don't shoot! Don't fire on us! We'll give up!" cried Happy Harry, and the two with the oars ceased pulling.

"Don't take any chances," urged Mr. Sharp in a low voice. "Keep between them and the shore. I'll cover them." Tom was steering from an auxiliary side wheel near the motor, and soon the *Arrow* had cut off the retreat of the men. They could not land and to row across the lake meant speedy capture.

"Well, what do you want of us?" growled Morse. "What right have you got to interfere with us in this fashion?"

"The best of right," answered Tom. "You'll find out when you're landed in jail."

"You can't arrest us!" sneered Happy Harry. "You're not an officer and you haven't any warrant."

Tom hadn't thought of that, and his chagrin showed in his face. Happy Harry was quick to see it.

"You'd better let us go," he threatened. "We can have you arrested for bothering us. You haven't any right to stop us, Tom Swift."

"Maybe he hasn't, but I have!" exclaimed John Sharp suddenly.

"You! Who are you?" demanded Featherton, *alias* Simpson, the man who had run the automobile that carried Tom away.

"Me. I'm a special deputy sheriff for this county," answered the balloonist simply. "Here's my badge," and, throwing back his coat, he displayed it. "You see I got the appointment in order to have some authority in the crowds that gather to watch me go up," he explained to Tom, who plainly showed his astonishment. "I found it very useful to be able to threaten arrest, but in this case I'll do more than threaten. You are my prisoners," he went on to the men in the boat, and he handled the shotgun as if he knew how to use it. "I'll take you into custody on complaint of Mr. Swift for robbery. Now will you go quietly or are you going to make a fuss?" and Mr. Sharp shut his jaw grimly.

"Well, seeing as how you have the drop on us, I guess we'll have to do as you say," admitted Happy Harry, *alias* Jim Burke. "But you can't prove anything against us. We haven't any ol Mr. Swift's property."

"Well, you know where it is then," retorted Tom quickly.

Under the restraining influence of the gun the

men made no resistance. While Mr. Sharp covered them, Tom towed their boat toward shore. Then, while the young inventor held the gun, the balloonist tied the hands and feet of the thieves in a most scientific manner, for what he did not know about ropes and knots was not worth putting into a book.

"Now, I guess they'll stay quiet for a while," remarked Mr. Sharp as he surveyed the crestfallen criminals. "I'll remain on guard here, Tom, while you go notify the nearest constable and we'll take them to jail. We bagged the whole lot as neatly as could be desired."

"No, you didn't get all of us!" exclaimed Happy Harry, and there was a savage anger in his tones.

"Keep quiet!" urged Morse.

"No, I'll not keep quiet! It's a shame that we have to take our medicine while that trimmer, Tod Boreck, goes free. He ought to have been with us, and he would be, only he's trying to get away with that sparkler!"

"Keep quiet," again urged Morse.

Tom was all attention. He had caught the word "sparkler," and he at once associated it with the occasion he had heard the men use it before. He felt that he was on the track of solving the mystery connected with his boat.

He looked at the men. They were the same four who had been involved in the former theft— Appleson, Featherton, Morse and Burke. Were there five of them? He recalled the man who had been caught tampering with his boat—the man who had tried to bid on the *Arrow* at the auction. Where was he?

"Boreck didn't get what he was after," resumed Happy Harry, "and I'm going to spoil his game for him. Say, kid," he went on to Tom, "look in the front part of your boat—where the gasoline tank is."

Tom felt his heart beating fast. At last he felt that he would solve the puzzle. He opened the forward compartment. To his disappointment it seemed as usual. Morse and the others were making a vain effort to silence Happy Harry.

"I don't see anything here," said Tom.

"No, because it's hidden in one of those blocks of wood you use for a brace," continued the man. "Which one it is, Boreck didn't know, so he pulled out two or three, only to be fooled each time. You must have shifted them, kid, from the way they were when *we* had the boat."

"I did," answered the young inventor, recollecting how he had taken out some of the braces and inserted new ones, then painted the interior of the compartment. "What is in the braces, anyhow?"

"The sparkler—a big diamond—in a hollow place in the wood, kid!" exclaimed Happy Harry, blurting out the words. "I'm not going to let Tod Boreck get away with it while we stay in jail."

"Take out all the braces that haven't been moved and have a look," suggested Mr. Sharp. Tom only had to remove two, those farthest back, for all the others had, at one time or another, been changed or taken away by the thief.

One of the blocks did not seem to have anything unusual about it, but at the sight of the other Tom could not repress a cry. It was the one that seemed to have had a hole bored in it and then plugged up again. He remembered his father noticing it on the occasion of overhauling the boat.

"The sparkler's in there," said the tramp as he saw the brace. "Boreck was after it several times, but he never pulled out the right one."

With his knife Tom dug out the putty that covered the round hole in the block. No sooner had he done so than there rolled out into his hand a white object. It was something done up in tissue paper, and as he removed the wrapper, there was a flash in the sunlight and a large, beautiful diamond was revealed. The mystery had been solved.

CHAPTER XXV

WINNING A RACE

"WHERE did this diamond come from?" demanded Mr. Sharp of the quartette of criminals.

"That's for us to know and you to find out," sneered Happy Harry. "I don't care as long as that trimmer Boreck didn't get it. He tried to do us out of our share."

"Well, I guess the police will make you tell," went on the balloonist. "Go for the constable, Tom."

Leaving his friend to guard the ugly men, who, for a time at least, were beyond the possibility of doing harm, Tom hurried off through the woods to the nearest village. There he found an officer and the gang was soon lodged in jail. The diamond was turned over to the authorities, who said they would soon locate the owner.

Nor were they long in doing it, for it appeared the gem was part of a large jewel robbery that had taken place some time before in a distant city. The Happy Harry gang, as the men came to be called, were implicated in it, though they got only a small share of the plunder. Search was made for Tod Boreck and he was captured about a week after his companions. Seeing that their game was up, the men made a partial confession, telling where Mr. Swift's goods had been secreted, and the inventor's valuable tools, papers and machinery were recovered, no damage having been done to them.

It developed that after the diamond theft, and when the gang still had possession of Mr. Hastings' boat, Boreck, sometimes called Murdock by his cronies, unknown to them, had secreted the jewel in one of the braces under the gasoline tank. He expected to get it out secretly, but the capture of the gang and the sale of the boat prevented this. Then he tried to buy the craft to take out the diamond, but Tom overbid him. It was Boreck who found Andy's bunch of keys and used one to open the compartment lock when Tom surprised him. The man did manage to remove some of the blocks, thinking he had the one with the diamond in it, but the fact of Tom changing them and painting the compartment deceived him. The gang hoped to get some valuables from Mr. Swift's shops, and, to a certain extent, succeeded after hanging around for several nights and following him to Sandport, but Tom eventually proved too much for them. Even stealing the *Ar-row*, which was taken to aid the gang in robbing Mr. Swift, did not succeed, and Boreck's plan then to get possession of the diamond fell through.

It was thought that the gang would get long terms in prison, but one night, during a violent storm, they escaped from the local jail and that was the last seen of them for some time.

A few days after the capture as Tom was in the boathouse making some minor repairs to the motor he heard a voice calling:

"Mistah Swift, am yo' about?"

"Hello, Rad, is that you?" he inquired, recognizing the voice of the colored owner of the mule Boomerang.

"Yais, sa, dat's me. I got a lettah fo' yo'. I were passing' de post-office an' de clerk asted me to brung it to you' 'case as how it's marked 'hurry,' an' he said he hadn't seen yo' to-day."

"That's right. I've been so busy I haven't had time to go for the mail," and Tom took the letter, giving Eradicate ten cents for his trouble.

"Ha, that's good!" exclaimed Tom as he read it.

"Hab some one done gone an' left yo' a fortune, Mistah Swift?" asked the negro.

"No, but it's almost as good. It's an invitation

to take part in the motor-boat races next week.
I'd forgotten all about them. I must get ready."

"Good land! Dat's all de risin' generation
t'inks about now," observed Eradicate, "racin'
an' goin' fast. Mah ole mule Boomerang am
good enough fo' me," and, shaking his head in a
woeful manner, Eradicate went on his way.

Tom told Mr. Sharp and his father of the proposed races of the Lanton Motor-Boat Club, and,
as it was required that two persons be in a craft
the size of the *Arrow*, the young inventor arranged for the balloonist to accompany him. Our
hero spent the next few days in tuning up his
motor and in getting the *Arrow* ready for the
contest.

The races took place on that side of Lake Carlopa near where Mr. Hastings lived, and he was
one of the officials of the club. There were several
classes, graded according to the horse-power of
the motors, and Tom found himself in a class with
Andy Foger.

"Here's where I beat you," boasted the red-
haired youth exultantly, though his manner toward Tom was more temperate than usual. Andy
had learned a lesson.

"Well, if you can beat me I'll give you credit for
it," answered Tom.

The first race was for high-powered craft, and

in this Mr. Hastings' new *Carlopa* won. Then came the trial of the small boats, and Tom was pleased to note that Miss Nestor was on hand in the tiny *Dot*.

"Good luck!" he called to her as he was adjusting his timer, for his turn would come soon. "Remember what I told you about the spark," for he had given her a few lessons.

"If I win it will be due to you," she called brightly.

She did win, coming in ahead of several confident lads who had better boats. But Miss Nestor handled the *Dot* to perfection and crossed the line a boat's length ahead of her nearest competitor.

"Fine!" cried Tom, and then came the warning gun that told him to get ready for his trial.

This was a five-mile race and had several entrants. The affair was a handicap one and Tom had no reason to complain of the rating allowed him.

"Crack!" went the starting pistol and away went Tom and one or two others who had the same allowance as did he. A little later the others started and finally the last class, including Andy Foger. The *Red Streak* shot ahead and was soon in the lead, for Andy and Sam had learned better how to handle their craft. Tom and Mr. Sharp were worried, but they stuck grimly to the race

and when the turning stake was reached Tom's
motor had so warmed up and was running so well
that he crept up on Andy. A mile from the final
mark Andy and Tom were on even terms, and
though the red-haired lad tried to shake off his
rival he could not. Andy's ignition system failed
him several times and he changed from batteries to
magneto and back again in the hope of getting a
little more speed out of the motor.

But it was not to be. A half mile away from
the finish Tom, who had fallen behind a little,
crept up on even terms. Then he slowly forged
ahead, and, a hundred rods from the stake, the
young inventor knew that the race was his. He
clinched it a few minutes later, crossing the line
amid a burst of cheers. The *Arrow* had beaten
several boats out of her own class and Tom was
very proud and happy.

"My, but we certainly did scoot along some!"
cried Mr. Sharp. "But that's nothing to how we'll
go when we build our airship, eh, Tom?" and he
looked at the flushed face of the lad.

"No, indeed," agreed the young inventor. "But
I don't know that we'll take part in any races in it.
We'll build it, however, as soon as we can solve
that one difficulty."

They did solve it, as will be told in the next
book of this series, to be called "Tom Swift and

His Airship; or, The Stirring Cruise of the *Red Cloud.*" They had some remarkable adventures in the wonderful craft, and solved the mystery of a great bank robbery.

This ended the contests of the motor-boats and the little fleet crowded up to the floats and docks, where the prizes were to be awarded. Tom received a handsome silver cup and Miss Nestor a gold bracelet.

"Now I want all the contestants, winners and losers, to come up to my house and have lunch," invited Mr. Hastings.

As Tom and the balloonist strolled up the walk to the handsome house Andy Foger passed them.

"You wouldn't have beaten me if my spark coil hadn't gone back on me," he said, somewhat sneeringly.

"Maybe," admitted Tom, and just then he caught sight of Mary Nestor. "May I take you in to lunch?" he asked.

"Yes," she said, "because you helped me to win," and she blushed prettily. And then they all sat down to the tables set out on the lawn, while Tom looked so often at Mary Nestor that Mr. Sharp said afterward it was a wonder he found time to eat. But Tom didn't care. He was happy.

THE END

THE TOM SWIFT SERIES

By VICTOR APPLETON

12mo. CLOTH. UNIFORM STYLE OF BINDING. COLORED WRAPPERS.

These spirited tales convey in a realistic way the wonderful advances in land and sea locomotion. Stories like these are impressed upon the memory and their reading is productive only of good.

TOM SWIFT AND HIS MOTOR CYCLE
Or Fun and Adventure on the Road

TOM SWIFT AND HIS MOTOR BOAT
Or The Rivals of Lake Carlopa

TOM SWIFT AND HIS AIRSHIP
Or The Stirring Cruise of the Red Cloud

TOM SWIFT AND HIS SUBMARINE BOAT
Or Under the Ocean for Sunken Treasure

TOM SWIFT AND HIS ELECTRIC RUNABOUT
Or The Speediest Car on the Road

TOM SWIFT AND HIS WIRELESS MESSAGE
Or The Castaways of Earthquake Island

TOM SWIFT AMONG THE DIAMOND MAKERS
Or The Secret of Phantom Mountain

TOM SWIFT IN THE CAVES OF ICE
Or The Wreck of the Airship

TOM SWIFT AND HIS SKY RACER
Or The Quickest Flight on Record

TOM SWIFT AND HIS ELECTRIC RIFLE
Or Daring Adventures in Elephant Land

TOM SWIFT IN THE CITY OF GOLD
Or Marvellous Adventures Underground

TOM SWIFT AND HIS AIR GLIDER
Or Seeking the Platinum Treasure

TOM SWIFT IN CAPTIVITY
Or A Daring Escape by Airship

TOM SWIFT AND HIS WIZARD CAMERA
Or The Perils of Moving Picture Taking

TOM SWIFT AND HIS GREAT SEARCHLIGHT
Or On the Border for Uncle Sam

TOM SWIFT AND HIS GIANT CANNON
Or The Longest Shots on Record

TOM SWIFT AND HIS PHOTO TELEPHONE
Or The Picture that Saved a Fortune

TOM SWIFT AND HIS AERIAL WARSHIP
Or The Naval Terror of the Seas

TOM SWIFT AND HIS BIG TUNNEL
Or The Hidden City of the Andes

GROSSET & DUNLAP, PUBLISHERS NEW YORK

THE MOVING PICTURE BOYS
SERIES
By VICTOR APPLETON

12mo. BOUND IN CLOTH.   ILLUSTRATED.   UNIFORM STYLE OF BINDING.

Moving pictures and photo plays are famous the world over, and in this line of books the reader is given a full description of how the films are made—the scenes of little dramas, indoors and out, trick pictures to satisfy the curious, soul-stirring pictures of city affairs, life in the Wild West, among the cowboys and Indians, thrilling rescues along the seacoast, the daring of picture hunters in the jungle among savage beasts, and the great risks run in picturing conditions in a land of earthquakes. The volumes teem with adventures and will be found interesting from first chapter to last.

THE MOVING PICTURE BOYS
Or Perils of a Great City Depicted.

THE MOVING PICTURE BOYS IN THE WEST
Or Taking Scenes Among the Cowboys and Indians.

THE MOVING PICTURE BOYS ON THE COAST
Or Showing the Perils of the Deep.

THE MOVING PICTURE BOYS IN THE JUNGLE
Or Stirring Times Among the Wild Animals.

THE MOVING PICTURE BOYS IN EARTHQUAKE LAND
Or Working Amid Many Perils.

THE MOVING PICTURE BOYS AND THE FLOOD
Or Perilous Days on the Mississippi.

THE MOVING PICTURE BOYS AT PANAMA
Or Stirring Adventures Along the Great Canal.

THE MOVING PICTURE BOYS UNDER THE SEA
Or The Treasure of the Lost Ship.

GROSSET & DUNLAP,   PUBLISHERS,   NEW YORK

THE OUTDOOR GIRLS SERIES
By LAURA LEE HOPE
Author of the "Bobbsey Twin Books" and "Bunny Brown"
Series.

12mo. BOUND IN CLOTH.   ILLUSTRATED.   UNIFORM STYLE OF BINDING.

These tales take in the various adventures participated in by several bright, up-to-date girls who love outdoor life. They are clean and wholesome, free from sensationalism, absorbing from the first chapter to the last.

THE OUTDOOR GIRLS OF DEEPDALE
Or Camping and Tramping for Fun and Health.

Telling how the girls organized their Camping and Tramping Club, how they went on a tour, and of various adventures which befell them.

THE OUTDOOR GIRLS AT RAINBOW LAKE
Or Stirring Cruise of the Motor Boat Gem.

One of the girls becomes the proud possessor of a motor boat and invites her club members to take a trip down the river to Rainbow Lake, a beautiful sheet of water lying between the mountains.

THE OUTDOOR GIRLS IN A MOTOR CAR
Or The Haunted Mansion of Shadow Valley.

One of the girls has learned to run a big motor car, and she invites the club to go on a tour to visit some distant relatives. On the way they stop at a deserted mansion and make a surprising discovery.

THE OUTDOOR GIRLS IN A WINTER CAMP
Or Glorious Days on Skates and Ice Boats.

In this story, the scene is shifted to a winter season. The girls have some jolly times skating and ice boating, and visit a hunters' camp in the big woods.

THE OUTDOOR GIRLS IN FLORIDA.
Or Wintering in the Sunny South.

The parents of one of the girls have bought an orange grove in Florida, and her companions are invited to visit the place. They take a trip into the interior, where several unusual things happen.

THE OUTDOOR GIRLS AT OCEAN VIEW
Or The Box that Was Found in the Sand.

The girls have great fun and solve a mystery while on an outing along the New England coast.

THE OUTDOOR GIRLS ON PINE ISLAND
Or A Cave and What it Contained.

A bright, healthful story, full of good times at a bungalow camp on Pine Island.

GROSSET & DUNLAP,   PUBLISHERS,   NEW YORK

THE GIRLS OF CENTRAL HIGH SERIES

By GERTRUDE W. MORRISON

12mo. BOUND IN CLOTH.   ILLUSTRATED.   UNIFORM STYLE OF BINDING.

Here is a series full of the spirit of high school life of to-day. The girls are real flesh-and-blood characters, and we follow them with interest in school and out. There are many contested matches on track and field, and on the water, as well as doings in the classroom and on the school stage. There is plenty of fun and excitement, all clean, pure and wholesome,

THE GIRLS OF CENTRAL HIGH
Or Rivals for all Honors.
A stirring tale of high school life, full of fun, with a touch of mystery and a strange initiation.

THE GIRLS OF CENTRAL HIGH ON LAKE LUNA
Or The Crew That Won.
Telling of water sports and fun galore, and of fine times in camp.

THE GIRLS OF CENTRAL HIGH AT BASKETBALL
Or The Great Gymnasium Mystery.
Here we have a number of thrilling contests at basketball and in addition, the solving of a mystery which had bothered the high school authorities for a long while.

THE GIRLS OF CENTRAL HIGH ON THE STAGE
Or The Play That Took the Prize.
How the girls went in for theatricals and how one of them wrote a play which afterward was made over for the professional stage and brought in some much-needed money,

THE GIRLS OF CENTRAL HIGH ON TRACK AND FIELD
Or The Girl Champions of the School League
This story takes in high school athletics in their most approved and up-to-date fashion. Full of fun and excitement.

THE GIRLS OF CENTRAL HIGH IN CAMP
Or The Old Professor's Secret.
The girls went camping on Acorn Island and had a delightful time at boating, swimming and picnic parties,

GROSSET & DUNLAP,   PUBLISHERS,   NEW·YORK

THE MOVING PICTURE GIRLS SERIES

By LAURA LEE HOPE

Author of "The Bobbsey Twins Series."

12mo. BOUND IN CLOTH. ILLUSTRATED. UNIFORM STYLE OF BINDING

The adventures of Ruth and Alice DeVere. Their father, a widower, is an actor who has taken up work for the "movies." Both girls wish to aid him in his work and visit various localities to act in all sorts of pictures.

THE MOVING PICTURE GIRLS
Or First Appearance in Photo Dramas.

Having lost his voice, the father of the girls goes into the movies and the girls follow. Tells how many "parlor dramas" are filmed.

THE MOVING PICTURE GIRLS AT OAK FARM
Or Queer Happenings While Taking Rural Plays.

Full of fun in the country, the haps and mishaps of taking film plays, and giving an account of two unusual discoveries.

THE MOVING PICTURE GIRLS SNOWBOUND
Or The Proof on the Film.

A tale of winter adventures in the wilderness, showing how the photo-play actors sometimes suffer.

THE MOVING PICTURE GIRLS UNDER THE PALMS
Or Lost in the Wilds of Florida.

How they went to the land of palms, played many parts in dramas before the camera; were lost, and aided others who were also lost.

THE MOVING PICTURE GIRLS AT ROCKY RANCH
Or Great Days Among the Cowboys.

All who have ever seen moving pictures of the great West will want to know just how they are made. This volume gives every detail and is full of clean fun and excitement.

THE MOVING PICTURE GIRLS AT SEA
Or a Pictured Shipwreck that Became Real.

A thrilling account of the girls' experiences on the water.

THE MOVING PICTURE GIRLS IN WAR PLAYS
Or The Sham Battles at Oak Farm.

The girls play important parts in big battle scenes and have plenty of hard work along with considerable fun.

GROSSET & DUNLAP,   PUBLISHERS,   NEW YORK

THE BOYS OF COLUMBIA HIGH
SERIES

By GRAHAM B. FORBES

Never was there a cleaner, brighter, more manly boy than Frank Allen, the hero of this series of boys' tales, and never was there a better crowd of lads to associate with than the students of the School. All boys will read these stories with deep interest. The rivalry between the towns along the river was of the keenest, and plots and counterplots to win the champions, at baseball, at football, at boat racing, at track athletics, and at ice hockey, were without number. Any lad reading one volume of this series will surely want the others.

THE BOYS OF COLUMBIA HIGH
Or The All Around Rivals of the School

THE BOYS OF COLUMBIA HIGH ON THE DIAMOND
Or Winning Out by Pluck

THE BOYS OF COLUMBIA HIGH ON THE RIVER
Or The Boat Race Plot that Failed

THE BOYS OF COLUMBIA HIGH ON THE GRIDIRON
Or The Struggle for the Silver Cup

THE BOYS OF COLUMBIA HIGH ON THE ICE
Or Out for the Hockey Championship

THE BOYS OF COLUMBIA HIGH IN TRACK ATH-
LETICS
Or A Long Run that Won

THE BOYS OF COLUMBIA HIGH IN WINTER SPORTS
Or Stirring Doings on Skates and Iceboats

12mo. Illustrated. Handsomely bound in cloth, with cover design and wrappers in colors.

GROSSET & DUNLAP,   PUBLISHERS,   NEW YORK